No Place for Me

Barthe DeClements

VIKING KESTREL

VIKING KESTREL
Viking Penguin Inc., 40 West 23rd Street, New York, New York 10010, U.S.A.
Penguin Books Ltd, 27 Wrights Lane, London W8 5TZ (Publishing & Editorial) and
Harmondsworth, Middlesex, England (Distribution & Warehouse)
Penguin Books Australia Ltd, Ringwood, Victoria, Australia
Penguin Books Canada Limited, 2801 John Street, Markham, Ontario, Canada L3R 1B4
Penguin Books (N.Z.) Ltd, 182–190 Wairau Road, Auckland 10, New Zealand

Copyright © Barthe DeClements, 1987
All rights reserved
First published in 1987 by Viking Penguin Inc.
Published simultaneously in Canada
Printed in the United States of America by Arcata Graphics, Fairfield, Pennsylvania
Set in Times Roman
1 2 3 4 5 91 90 89 88 87

Library of Congress Cataloging-in-Publication Data
DeClements, Barthe.   No place for me.
Summary: Copper Jones is shuttled back and forth
between her relatives while her mother is drying out
in a rehabilitation center; but when she is sent
to live with her Aunt Maggie, who is a witch, she
learns that even seventh graders have some power.
[1. Witches—fiction. 2. Alcoholism—Fiction.
3. Aunts—Fiction] I. Title PZ7.D3584Nn
1987   [Fic]   87-10605   ISBN 0-670-81908-5

This book is for Melody

ACKNOWLEDGMENTS

I would like to give thanks to Melody Toth, who was my resourceful guide into the world of twelve-year-olds. And thanks to my daughter, Nicole Southard, and my son, Christopher Greimes, for their critiques of the manuscript in progress. And a special thanks to Claire Norcross, whose healing skills and gentle acceptance of people were the inspiration for these qualities in Maggie.

No Place for Me

Chapter
1

SITTING ON THE DECK OVERLOOKING LAKE WASHING-ton, I felt the morning sun warm me into a lazy daze. Snatches of the phone conversation in the apartment drifted out to me. Jeff, my stepfather, was obviously trying to talk my aunt Judith into letting me stay with her. He must be going on a business trip, I thought, as I took a sip from my glass of orange juice.

He didn't sound like he was having much luck. And that was fine with me. I hoped I'd get to stay with my friend Johanna while he was gone.

Jeff opened the sliding glass door. "Copper, I'm trying to find a place for you to live. Your uncle Raymond's running for state senator, so your aunt Judith feels they'll be too busy. Would you like me to call your aunt Dorothy or your father's sister next?"

"You don't have to bother," I told him. "I'm sure Johanna's mother will let me stay with them."

"I mean a place for you to be permanently."

Permanently? I whipped my head around to stare at him.

He was studying the tips of his shoes. "Or at least until your mother's treatment is over."

This didn't make sense. "What's the big deal? Last time she went, it was only ten days."

"That's true, but the center she's in now likes to keep the patients six weeks. And I'm not just going on a sales trip, Copper. I'm leaving to work out of the Portland office."

"For how long?"

"I don't know how long."

"Maybe longer than it takes my mom to be cured?"

"Possibly."

"You're dumping my mom," I said.

"That isn't it at all." He had stopped examining his shoes and was looking out over the water. "Shall I call Dorothy next?"

I shook the ice around in my glass, trying to give myself time to think.

"Well?" There was an impatient edge to Jeff's voice.

"What are you going to do with this apartment?" I asked.

"I'll put everything in storage, and your mother can decide where she wants to live when she gets out."

"You *are* dumping her."

"Copper, I'm not going to get in an argument with you. This is Sunday and I need to get you settled today. Do you have any objections to my calling Dorothy and Tom?"

"They only have a small house and three girls. There isn't any room for me there."

"Would you rather stay with your father's sister?"

"Aunt Margo?" I thumped my glass down on the wooden table beside me. "You've got to be kidding. She's a witch."

"Well, I'll call Dorothy, then." He went into the apartment while I sat in my chair with alarm building inside of me. Jeff's sales pitch on the phone made it obvious that nobody wanted me. I felt like a scum.

One small hope flickered in my head. If Aunt Dorothy said no, maybe Jeff would take me to Portland with him. He wouldn't put me with Aunt Margo. She was too weird. A witch. A *real* witch.

My dad died when I was seven. When he was alive, he liked to visit his sister. My mom would always make a big fuss. She said she didn't want her kid around anybody who practiced witchcraft. Every once in a while, Dad got his way, though. I never let go of my mom's hand once we were inside Aunt Margo's house. I didn't want to get popped into a cage like Hansel and Gretel.

When Jeff came back onto the deck, he said, "Let's get you packed."

I didn't move my head, but I shot a glance at him out of the corner of my eye. "For where?"

"For Dorothy's."

"You aren't wasting any time getting rid of me, are you?"

He walked over to where I was sitting and pulled a canvas chair around so that he would be facing me. After he sat down, he reached out and took my hand. "Maybe you're too young to understand this, but I'll try. I will always love your mother, but I don't know if I can live with her again. I need to take responsibility in the business I'm in, and I can't do it and party with her, too."

"Maybe she won't like to party so much when she gets cured."

He nodded solemnly. "Maybe."

There wasn't much I could do then, except cry. I knew my mom and he knew my mom. Crying wasn't going to help, so I pulled my hand away and got up. "How much am I supposed to pack?"

"Pack enough for two or three months."

Halfway to the sliding glass doors, I stopped and turned around. "Two or three months! She's already been there a week."

"Well, pack plenty, then. I'm storing the rest. You're starting school in a week and a half, remember."

School. I wouldn't be going to school with my friends in Seattle. I'd be out in the sticks in Marysville, where I wasn't even wanted.

At the Marysville exit, Jeff pulled off the freeway and headed east into the town. The "town" consisted of a long street of one-story buildings, Pay 'n Pak, skating rink, Kentucky Fried Chicken, used-car lot, K-Mart. "Just where I always dreamed of living," I muttered. My hands were pressed against my stomach, which might as well have been riding on the car axle.

Jeff kept his eyes on the road. He drove down State

Street, turned on Shoultes, and curved around until he came to the Saxtons' driveway. Sarah was sitting on the front steps. While Jeff was parking, she twisted her head around and hollered, "They're here!" Nobody came out the screen door to greet us.

Sarah followed us into the living room, chattering away. "Kim and Brenda are upstairs getting everything moved around. Mom's in the kitchen making a pie. In case you want to stay for dinner, Uncle Jeff." She looked up at him with her round, blue eyes.

He gave her a weak smile. "No, I have to get back. I've got a lot of moving to do, too."

Sarah grabbed my arm. "You're going to sleep in my room."

What! Sarah's eight years old. Brenda's eleven, and Kim's thirteen. Since I'm twelve, I figured I'd be with Kim. I shook loose of Sarah and took the stairs two at a time.

Brenda was in the upper hall lugging a pile of clothes toward Kim's room.

"How come you're moving out of Sarah's room?" I asked her. "I thought you and Kim fought so much your mom didn't want you two together."

"We gotta make a place for you," Brenda told me. "Grab that, quick."

I caught the flowered pants slipping off the pile and carried them into Kim's room. Kim was pushing a nightstand across the floor. Her black eyes looked burning mad.

5

"Why is Brenda moving in here?" I said. "I could just move in with you."

"It wasn't my idea," Kim snarled and gave the stand another angry shove.

I beat a path back downstairs. Aunt Dorothy and Jeff were in the living room. Jeff was sitting on the davenport making out a check. I planted myself in front of my aunt's chair.

"It isn't necessary to move everybody around for me. I can just bunk with Kim while I'm here, OK?" I put on my mother's charming smile and waited for Aunt Dorothy to agree with me.

She didn't. "The girls have already made the change. And Sarah's looking forward to having you with her. Right, Sarah?"

Sarah was leaning on her mother's chair. She gave me a toothy grin. I ignored her.

"But, Aunt Dorothy, this is all too much trouble. I'll help Brenda take her clothes back to her and Sarah's room and then I'll just take my stuff up to Kim's. Kim and I will get along fine." I was hoping the part about getting along fine would cinch it. It didn't.

"No, just leave it like I've planned. You move into Sarah's room."

Jeff stood up, handed the check to Aunt Dorothy, and said to me, "Come on, Copper, let's get your things out of the car."

Sarah tagged after us as we went out the screen door. She stood at my elbow while I waited for Jeff to open the trunk. "This is going to be fun, Copper."

"For who?" I took the boxes Jeff handed me, and piled them on the curb. Sarah took two small ones up to the porch.

When the trunk was empty, Jeff pulled a twenty-dollar bill out of his wallet and gave it to me. "You might need to buy some things for yourself," he said.

I tried one last hope. "Maybe I could come to Portland when you get settled there. Do you think so?"

"I think you'll be fine here." He bent and kissed me on the cheek.

I couldn't help it. I started to cry.

Jeff patted my shoulder. "You'll be all right. You'll be all right."

I put my hand over my mouth to stop it from trembling. "But what about Mom?"

"I'll talk to your mother." He gave me one more pat, got in the car, and drove away.

Chapter
2

I STARED DOWN AT THE DINNER PLATE UNCLE TOM HAD filled for me. The heavy, deserted feeling sickening my stomach made it almost impossible to eat. I picked at a few green beans.

"Please pass the butter," Aunt Dorothy said from across the table. She was wearing a baby-blue, sleeveless dress with ruffles that went from her shoulders to her waist. I thought it looked dumb with her gray-streaked hair. My mom would never let her red hair get gray.

"Don't you like your dinner?" Aunt Dorothy asked me.

"Oh. Yes, it's excellent." I concentrated on cutting my slice of ham into little pieces. I hadn't meant to get caught staring at her.

"The badminton net is set up in the backyard," my uncle Tom told us. "I thought you girls might like to play a game after dinner."

"Neat!" Sarah said. "You can be my partner, Copper."

I felt Aunt Dorothy eyeing me, waiting for my response. "OK," I agreed and stuck my fork in the mushy potato salad.

Fortunately, after two sets, Brenda decided she wanted to play with me, so Kim had to take Sarah. That didn't last long. Kim doesn't like to get beaten. The third time Sarah batted the air, Kim threw down her racket and called it quits.

Inside the house, she went straight for the phone to talk to one of her girlfriends. I wandered around the living room for a while, then went upstairs to unpack the rest of my junk. Sarah tagged after me.

While I put my stuff away, she watched me from the top of her bed. "You can't stick that poster on the wall."

I turned around and looked at her. "Who says I can't?"

"Mom."

"What are you talking about? Kim's got posters in her room."

"Ya, but Dad just painted these walls."

"She's right, Copper." Brenda came in the door with a pleased little smile on her face. "That's why I wanted out of here."

I plunked down on the bed that was supposed to be mine. It smelled funny. My aunt could have washed the quilt to go with the clean walls.

"Let me see who you've got." Brenda came over and took the poster out of my hand. "Oh, Rob Lowe! This is kind of old, isn't it? He doesn't have his hair that long anymore." She tilted her head to the side. "He's gorgeous, though. I love his earring." She handed the picture back. "Too bad you can't put it up."

"No big thing." I rolled up the poster and stashed it in

the corner of the closet, took my *Bop* magazine out of the box I'd shoved under the hanging clothes, went over to the bed, and stretched out. Brenda stayed behind, rummaging in my junk.

"Oh, you've got *16.* And *Teen Idols*! Don't you love Kirk Cameron? Can I read a couple of these?"

"I don't care." I watched Sarah get off her bed and go to my box. I wanted to tell her to stay out of it, but decided to wait until Brenda left.

She left when her mother came in to tell us it was time to turn off the lights. Brenda put back the magazines she was reading. Sarah dumped hers on the floor before she crawled into bed. That did it.

I stood over her in my pajamas. "Get up and put my magazines away."

She dug her head into the pillow. "They'll be all right until tomorrow."

"Put them back in the closet. You don't have any business getting into my stuff."

She turned to face the wall. "Nothing's going to hurt them. I'll put them away tomorrow morning."

I yanked her covers off. "You'll do it now!"

She got up slowly, gathered up the magazines, and put them in the box. "I'm going to tell Mom I don't want you in my room," she said as she got back in bed.

I didn't bother to answer her. But when I pulled the quilt over my shoulders, the funny smell got worse and I asked her, "Whose bed did this use to be?"

"That was mine. I took Brenda's when she left. Mom said I could. Anyway, they both have new mattresses."

"Do you wet your bed?"

"No, I don't!" Her indignant tone sounded loud in the dark room.

"Well, how come this bed stinks, then?"

"You're probably smelling yourself." She giggled at her little joke.

"It's not me," I told her. "It's this blanket. Somebody must have peed on it."

I rolled the quilt down from my face and pulled the sheet around my chin so the smell wouldn't get to me so bad. After a while I started wondering what my mother was doing.

Sarah must have been thinking, too. Suddenly she said into the night, "My mom says you try to manipulate people just like your mom does."

"So?"

"What does 'manipulate' mean?"

"Who cares? Go to sleep."

"I asked Kim, and she says it means trying to make people do what you want them to do."

"Big deal. Go to sleep."

"Is that what—"

"Listen, your mother is my mother's oldest sister. So your mom's saying mean things about her own sister. Now *shut up* or I'll come over and shut you up."

She shut up.

I didn't fall asleep for a long time. I just lay there feeling more alone than I'd ever felt in my life. And worrying about what my mom would do when she found out Jeff had split. I hoped it wouldn't start her drinking again.

In the morning, I gathered up my dirty underclothes and took them down to Aunt Dorothy. She was at the stove pouring coffee into a mug. "I didn't see a hamper in the bathroom," I told her. "Where do you want me to put my laundry?"

She looked at the clothes I had in my hand. "Oh, stick them in the washing machine. I'll do them later."

She moved over to the counter for some toast, and I moved along with her. "The quilt on my bed is pretty dirty. Do you want me to bring that down, too, so we can wash it?"

"The quilt? No. The quilt would have to go to the cleaners."

My cousins were sitting around the breakfast table. I sat down with them and picked up one of the boxes of cereal and shook it. It was empty. I reached over for the unopened one. Sarah grabbed it from me. "It's my turn to get the prize."

Kim leaned across the table and snatched the box out of Sarah's hands. "No it isn't, stupid. You had it last time."

"No I didn't. Brenda did. Give me—"

"That's enough!" Aunt Dorothy stalked across the room and pulled out the empty chair at the end of the table. "Any more arguing and I'll throw the prize in the garbage."

Kim quietly proceeded to open the box and fish through the cereal for a little plastic-wrapped package. Sarah's lips turned in over her big teeth as she watched her sister take out a silver-colored ring with a gold-colored heart at the center. Kim handed me the cereal box and tossed the ring toward Sarah's bowl. "Here, you can have the tin thing."

After Sarah put the ring on, she spread out her fingers. "There. I think it looks pretty good."

Kim raised one eyebrow at me, held a hand up to her left ear, and pretended to blow air through her head by flapping her other hand toward her right ear. I laughed. Kim is the only one of the cousins who looks like anything. She has wavy, black hair that she bunches up into a mane at the top of her head with a double-locked comb. And she wears cute clothes. Brenda always wears flowered pants or striped jeans, which make her fat stomach look fatter. Nothing looks good on Sarah. She's skinny, with big teeth and thin, blond hair like her mother.

When Aunt Dorothy finished her toast and coffee, she announced that she was going grocery shopping. "Do you girls want to go with me?"

"There's nothing else to do," Kim said.

I got up from the table and started stacking the cereal bowls. "This would be a good time to drop the quilt off at the cleaners, wouldn't it?"

"No," Aunt Dorothy told me. "I don't have the money for that. Just leave the quilt be for now."

Silently I finished clearing off the rest of the table. The cousins split upstairs. I guessed they were sticking me with the dishes.

While the hot water poured into the sink, I did my

thinking. Aunt Dorothy probably didn't have anything like Woolite, but shampoo should work in cold water. If the quilt couldn't go in the washing machine, it could go in the bathtub.

When Brenda came in the kitchen to tell me they were ready to leave, I said I thought I'd stay home and wash my hair. Aunt Dorothy came in a few seconds after Brenda left. "Are you sure you don't want to go with us? Those dishes can be left until we get back."

"No," I said. "My hair's filthy. I'll feel better after I get in the shower."

She stood there uncertainly a minute and then said, "Well, we won't be long."

I was hoping she would be. As soon as I heard the car start up, I dashed upstairs, took off my clothes, grabbed the quilt off the bed, and headed for the bathroom. At last I'd get that stinky thing clean.

I shampooed my hair first, letting the water pile up in the tub. After I got out, I turned on the cold water and dumped in the quilt. I tried to hold it under the waterline, but it kept bubbling to the surface. Finally I got back in the tub and stamped it down.

It was a real mess getting the quilt rinsed off, and a bigger mess trying to wring it out. There was water on the floor, water on the toilet seat, and piles of water still in the quilt. The quilt didn't look too good either. The insides were sort of smashed together like wet cat fur.

I mopped up the bathroom with a towel, got dressed, and lugged the quilt and towel downstairs. I put the towel in the top of the washing machine and stuffed the quilt in the dryer. While the wet, slimy thing thumped around and around, I stood there worrying, afraid I would ruin it. I decided I better take it out in the sun and not risk shrinking it in the dryer.

After I'd spread it on the ground in the Saxtons' little backyard, I squatted down to flap the corners in the air. After flapping and flapping and turning and turning, spots on the cover started to dry. The insides were still pretty soggy, though. I picked up the quilt and twirled it around until my arms ached.

There was the sound of a car pulling up in front of the house! Panic shot through me. I flew in the back door, dashed up the stairs, spread the quilt on the bed, and fluffed it up the best I could. By the time the cousins came upstairs, I was innocently blow-drying my hair in the bathroom.

Sarah was supposed to go to bed earlier than the rest of us girls. At nine-thirty, when I came in, I found her sitting on my bed with one of my rock magazines. "This quilt's wet," she said.

"I probably was lying on it after my shower," I told her. "And, anyway, get over on your side of the room. And don't borrow my magazines unless you ask me."

"I wasn't hurting them," she mumbled, climbing in her own bed.

When I got in mine, the damp sheets stuck to me. But at least the stink was gone.

Chapter
3

IT TOOK ABOUT A WEEK FOR THE QUILT TO DRY. I WAS nervous about it the whole time. I didn't know where I'd go if my aunt got mad at me. I sure wasn't going to live with a witch.

When Saturday came and we changed our beds, I told Sarah I'd take the dirty sheets down to the washing machine. I wanted to mix them up good so Aunt Dorothy wouldn't notice that mine were a bit damp. She didn't seem to. At least, she didn't say anything about it.

What she did say was that she had to go to the dentist and she'd drop us off at the Everett Mall if we'd like.

"Aw right!" Kim said. "Can we have some spare change to buy a magazine?"

"No, but the three of you can each choose a pair of school pants. Get them in the Triangle Shop, and I'll pay for them when I pick you up. Copper, I imagine your mother will get your school clothes later."

She didn't have to explain. I didn't expect her to buy me pants.

"And be sure they're all long enough," my aunt added. "I don't want you growing out of them before Christmas."

We were finishing up our lunch, and Kim put her fork on the table with a thump. "*Mom,* if you take pant legs down after you wear them, a crease shows where the old hem was. I don't wanna look like a scum."

"Well, Sarah's already grown an inch this summer. See that hers and Brenda's are long enough, then."

"Why me?" Brenda asked. "I don't wanna look like a scum, either."

"You already do," Kim told her.

Aunt Dorothy's head jerked sharply, and Kim threw up her hands. "Only kidding."

The dressing room was so crowded I had to stand while my cousins tried on their pants. After watching Brenda struggle to zip the fifth pair up over her fat stomach, I said, "It's too stuffy in here. I'll meet you guys at the earring counter in Jay Jacobs."

Jay Jacobs has wild earrings. I picked out some antique-gold-colored hoops with leaves swinging from the bottom. I held them up to my ears when Kim and her sisters came in. "What do you think?"

"Cool," Kim said.

Brenda nodded. "The hoops match your hair."

While I was paying for the earrings, Sarah was jumping up and down. "Let's go to Spencer's next! Let's go to Spencer's!"

"All right," Kim said. "Just stop pulling on me."

As soon as we were in Spencer's, Sarah rushed over to the phone display and plunked on the keys of an imitation toy piano. "Those are the phone buttons, stupid," Brenda told her. Brenda picked up the back of a Garfield cat and its eyes opened. "Copper, Copper, are you there?" she said into the receiver.

I was looking over a small black pay phone. It cost more money than I had left, and anyway, there probably wasn't a jack in Sarah's room.

"Hey, you guys, look at this!" Sarah was in the next aisle trying on a yellow plastic hard hat. It had holders on each side for soda cans and a sipping tube hanging down the front.

"Neat," Brenda said, and we all joined Sarah.

I found a white hard hat on the bottom shelf. Besides the soda can holders on the sides, it had a blue light and a siren on top with a speaker attached to a wire. Sarah reached over and pushed one of the buttons on the speaker and the blue light turned on and twirled around while the sound of a siren filled the store.

Brenda and Kim shoved Sarah toward the posters while I took a quick look at the front counter. Fortunately, the clerk was busy at the cash register and didn't seem to be paying any attention to the noise.

The sales sticker on the bottom of the hat said $15.19. I had just enough money left. After I bought the hat, I joined my cousins at the poster rack. Sarah took one look at my big package, and her upper lip drooped down over her horse's teeth. "Lucky."

It was the first thing she told her mom, when we met her in the Triangle Shop. "Copper's so lucky. She got a pair of earrings and a hat that carries pop."

Aunt Dorothy looked at me questioningly.

"Jeff gave me twenty dollars before he left," I explained.

"Well, if you want to spend your money on junk, I guess that's your business." She patted Sarah's shoulder. "I think I can spring for some ice cream cones at Bresler's before we go home."

Good, I thought. I was starved. Lunch had been canned spaghetti, which I hate.

At Bresler's, Sarah marched up and down the counter peering into the ice cream buckets. I swear she looked into all thirty-three flavors before she decided on fresh peach. I was standing back reading the lists on the wall. I sort of wanted lemon ice, but I also like maple nut. I like fresh peach, too.

Brenda had already chosen chocolate fudge, and Kim had chosen chocolate mint. Aunt Dorothy ordered my cousins' three flavors and added a plain vanilla for herself. I had been waiting for her to ask me what I wanted, and when she paid the clerk, I was startled. I thought maybe she'd made a mistake and forgotten me until she turned around holding the vanilla cone the clerk had given her. "Aren't you going to get any ice cream for yourself, Copper?"

"Oh. Oh, no," I said. "I'm not hungry."

I slowly followed my cousins and aunt out to the parking lot. I guessed Aunt Dorothy thought I still had some money. Or she was giving me a little lesson for buying all those things for myself and nothing for her daughters. Anyway, my empty stomach sank under the feeling that she didn't like me much.

When we got to the car, there was the usual big fight over who got to sit in the front and who got window seats. I didn't say a word, and for that I got squashed between Sarah and Brenda in the backseat. As we drove along, I looked straight ahead, trying not to see Sarah lick her creamy mound of ice cream or smell Brenda's chocolate fudge.

"Aunt Dorothy." I leaned forward so she could hear me. "I meant that the other girls could take turns wearing my hard hat, too."

She kept her eyes on the road, but nodded her head. "That's fine."

"Wow, hold my cone, Brenda." Sarah passed it to her behind my back, bent down, picked up my biggest package, and yanked the hard hat out. I didn't dare say a word as she put the hat on her head and pulled the speaker box down.

The blue light flashed. The sound of the siren filled the air. Aunt Dorothy yanked the car to the side of the road, causing the truck driver behind us to slam on his brakes. She looked around wildly. "Is it the police or an ambulance?"

"It's just Sarah, Mom," Kim told her.

"Sarah, turn that thing off," Aunt Dorothy ordered and shot me an angry look for good measure. Why? It wasn't my fault.

Sarah sat quietly with my hat on, licking and licking and licking her peach ice cream. I wanted to snatch the cone out of her paws and gobble it down.

When Brenda crunched up the last of her cone, she pulled her pants out of the sack. "I don't know if I want five-pocket jeans. I think I liked the tapered pants better."

"Look like a pumpkin on sticks, I don't care," Kim said.

I cared. I was glad Kim had talked her into the jeans— in case I had to be seen with Brenda. "Where do we go to school, anyway?" I asked.

"You and I go to the middle school," Brenda told me.

"*We* do? Where does Kim go?"

Kim turned around to face us. "I'm in eighth grade. I go to the junior high." She sounded pleased with herself.

"But seventh graders go to junior high, too," I said.

"Not in Marysville." Kim turned back around, and I slunk down over my empty stomach and listened to it growl the rest of the way to my aunt's house.

Chapter
4

JEFF HAD ALWAYS MADE MOM AND ME A SPECIAL SUN-
day breakfast. Except for Uncle Tom eating with us, Sunday was like any other day at the Saxtons', Lucky Charms
or Rice Krispies. While I was pouring milk into my bowl,
Aunt Dorothy brought up the subject of haircuts.

"School starts on Wednesday, so we better get the bar-
bershop going this morning." She took a squint-eyed ap-
praisal of me. "Copper, your bangs are even longer than
Sarah's. Are you going to have them cut or would you like
me to do it?"

I felt my face warm up with the memory of the ice
cream cones. "I don't have any money left," I said.

"I'll do you after Brenda, then." She was folding her
napkin and placing it next to her plate. "Kim, what about
you? Your hair's looking pretty shaggy."

"No, that's OK, Mom. I can do my own." Kim went
on up to her room. Uncle Tom headed for the living room
to watch the baseball game. Brenda and I started clearing
the table while Aunt Dorothy got Sarah settled on a stool
in the middle of the kitchen.

"Now, don't hack my bangs all off like you usually do," Sarah told her mother.

"Hold still and I won't have to." After she wrapped a dish towel around Sarah's neck, Aunt Dorothy picked up her kitchen shears. Just as she took a snip, Sarah started to protest some more.

"Oh, oh," my aunt said. She'd cut a wedge of hair above Sarah's left eyebrow.

"What did you do?" Sarah cried out.

"I told you to hold still. Now hold still."

I took little glances at the progress as Brenda and I went to and from the table to the sink. Each time I looked, Sarah's bangs were higher, until there was just a fringe of hair above a big, white strip of forehead. When her mother was finished with her, Sarah ripped off the towel and dashed for the bathroom mirror. We could hear her squalling while Aunt Dorothy got dumb Brenda to sit on the stool.

I wiped the last of the breakfast dishes. "Uh, I guess I won't have my hair cut today, Aunt Dorothy. I'll go on upstairs with Kim."

"Suit yourself," Aunt Dorothy said.

I found Kim sitting at her dressing table in her room combing out her long, black hair. She glanced at me and smiled. "You got smart."

"Well, your mom sort of butchered . . . I mean . . ."

"She always butchers. Here." Kim picked up a pair of scissors from her dressing table. "Can you trim my split ends? Just the ends, though."

While I carefully cut the frayed tips of Kim's hair, I thought about what I was going to do with mine. The only thing I could come up with was a visit to my mother. When I was about finished with Kim's split ends, Brenda bounced into the room. She didn't look too bad. All her mom had done was cut her hair unevenly above her shoulders. Lucky for her she didn't have bangs.

I gave Kim back the scissors and headed downstairs to tackle my aunt. I found her in the living room watching the game with Uncle Tom. I politely waited until a commercial came on the TV.

"Aunt Dorothy, do you suppose you could take me to visit my mother?"

"Well, I guess so. But I don't know just when." Her eye was half on me and half on the tube.

I gave Uncle Tom what I hoped was my mom's brilliant smile and then went at Aunt Dorothy again. "I'd really like to see her. Do you suppose you could take me today or—"

She interrupted me. "We've got a roast in the oven."

"Or tomorrow?" I made my voice sound as sweet as possible.

"Tomorrow's Labor Day," she said flatly.

"I realize that, but . . ." I desperately tried to think up another attack.

Uncle Tom saved me. "That might be a nice holiday drive. We could stop and have a picnic at the Skykomish River on the way back."

"Well, if the whole family's going out together, we

can take you tomorrow," Aunt Dorothy agreed.

I bobbed my head at her. "Thank you. Thank you very much," I said and gave Uncle Tom another big smile before I left the room.

While climbing up the stairs, I thought fast. My mom spends every cent she gets her hands on. The chance of her still having any money after she'd been out in that center for two weeks was pretty slight.

If she was broke, I could still go for her I. Magnin credit card. She'd let me use that once when she was trying on shoes in Magnin's and didn't want to stop to take me up to the beauty salon. I hoped there'd be enough change in the bottom of her purse for bus fare to Seattle.

I slipped my hand slowly along the banister. Things at my aunt's house were a lot different than they had been at mine. All I used to have to do for cash was wait until one of my mom's parties was in full swing and then go in the living room to ask her for movie money. Every other man in the place would reach in his wallet and say to me, "Here, Copper, here," and then say to my mother, "I've got it, Cassandra." Each time I'd leave my living room loaded with the bills I'd collected. My mom never remembered the next day.

At the top of the stairs, I pushed open the door to Kim's room and saw that she and Brenda were trying on outfits for school. "That red turtleneck looks cute on you," I told Kim.

She tilted her head at her dressing table mirror. "Hmm, if it isn't hot out Wednesday. Trouble is you can never tell ahead of time if it will be boiling or raining." She pulled her turtleneck off, plunked it on the bed, and picked a T-shirt off the floor. "So what are you going to do about your hair?"

"Get it cut Tuesday."

"How're you going to manage that?"

"Your folks are driving me over to see my mother tomorrow. Your dad wants us to have a picnic on the way back."

"Aw right. Let's get them to stop at a place where we see some guys, OK?"

"OK," I agreed. "We'll point out the 'prettiest place.' "

Kim took the clothes off her bed and hung them in the closet. Brenda still stood in a pile of flowered and striped jeans. I hoped she'd have brains enough to wear plain ones if I had to walk to school with her the first day.

"You'll be loaded after you see your mom, I suppose," Brenda said.

"Either that or I'll get her I. Magnin credit card."

"I. Magnin's! You're not going to get your hair cut there?" Kim asked.

"Well." I walked over to her dressing table and fluffed my hair in the mirror. "That's where my mother gets hers done. She says my hair is my best feature."

"I've never even been in Magnin's," Brenda said.

"It's neat." I left the mirror and headed for their door. "The rest rooms have marble floors and marble walls."

After I closed the door, I stood quietly outside. Brenda's mimicking my voice—" 'My mother says my hair's my best feature' "—didn't bother me. But what Kim said back made me cringe.

Kim said, "Everybody knows her mom's a drunk."

Chapter
5

WHILE UNCLE TOM DROVE UP THE TREE-LINED LANE TO
the entrance of the alcohol treatment center, Aunt Dorothy was deciding to visit my mom with me. My cousins
and uncle wanted to go off to find a picnic place. I wasn't
too comfortable about having my aunt with me. I wasn't
even too comfortable about going inside the long, brick
building. I hate hospitals. They seem like scary, hurting
places.

The center's lobby was nice enough. It had a thick blue
rug, black leather couches, lamps, and vases of flowers. A
receptionist was at a polished desk to the side of the front
door. Aunt Dorothy asked her to ring for my mom.

Mom rushed up to us in a flurry of jangling bracelets
and rich perfume. After she hugged me, she held me away
from her by my shoulders. "You need a haircut, Copper-
baby."

"I know," I told her. "That's why I'm here."

She made her face into a fake, pitiful pout. "You didn't
want to see me?"

I patted her hand. "Yes, I wanted to see my very own mother."

"You better." She put her arms around me and Aunt Dorothy and led us down the hall.

In the room, Mom and Aunt Dorothy sat in the two easy chairs and talked about Uncle Raymond's race for state senator. I perched on the bed and stroked the pink and purple satin pillows piled on the bedspread until Mom turned to me suddenly. "I don't see why you didn't ask Dorothy to get your hair cut."

"I offered to cut her hair," Aunt Dorothy said. "Copper also had twenty dollars from Jeff."

Mom's eyes narrowed at the word "Jeff." I figured I'd better lead the conversation into safe territory fast. "Well, I thought you'd want me to go to your Nanette. So I waited until I could see you." I held up one of the pillows. "They sure put neat colors in this place. You're lucky to be here."

"Lucky! Lucky!" Her voice rose in volume, and the old, sick fear seeped into my stomach.

"I . . . I just meant it's a pretty room."

"It should be," she snapped. "It cost enough."

"Isn't Jeff paying the bill?" Aunt Dorothy asked.

My mom was building up her rage and ignored her sister. "Copper, just how would you like to be stuck way out here in this 'pretty room'? Where the drinks are doctored to make you vomit all over yourself?"

"It would be a drag," I agreed, keeping a smile on my face. She kept a scowl on hers, so I hurried on to distract her. "Hey, you know what I did with the twenty dollars? I bought this hard hat that has a blue light on top. When you push a button, the light comes on and a siren screams. Sarah pushed the button when Aunt Dorothy was driving, and a truck almost bashed into the back of our car when Aunt Dorothy pulled over." I lay back on the bed and laughed loudly, hoping to get my mom to laugh, too.

She didn't. "Well, that's too bad for you, then. You should have saved the twenty dollars for a haircut. I'm not allowed to have money here, so you'll just have to go around looking like a shaggy dog."

Aunt Dorothy leaned over toward Mom to get her attention. "Cassandra, is Jeff still supporting you?"

"What difference does it make?"

"I just wondered. . . . How long do you plan to be in this place?"

"Jeff said he gave you a check for Copper's room and board." Mom's face was scrunched into hard, tight lines. "Didn't he give you enough?"

Aunt Dorothy waved her hands in front of her chest. "Oh, I didn't mean that. Really. I was worried about how you were going to get by."

That didn't relax my mom's face one bit. I sat up and bounced a pink pillow into the air to distract her. "Hey, hey, I've got a great idea." I reached for a purple pillow and threw that way up, too, so Mom's eyes would have to follow it. "I've got the perfect way to get my hair cut, and it won't cost any money. Where's your purse, Mom?"

While she was still looking confused by my juggling, I

dropped the pillows, scrambled up, and went for her purse on the dresser. "I can use your I. Magnin card, OK? And go to our old beauty parlor and get my hair done right, OK? And look, you've got a whole bunch of change in the bottom of your purse. That will get me down to Seattle on the bus, right?" After I stuffed the money and card in my jeans pocket, I went over to give her a hug. She didn't give me one back, but she didn't ask for the card back, either.

Aunt Dorothy stood up. "We better get going. Tom should be out in front waiting by now." She bent down, pecked her sister on the cheek, and headed for the door.

I stood for a minute by Mom's chair, twisting a lock of her curly red hair around my finger. "I miss you."

Just as Mom looked up at me, Aunt Dorothy stopped in the doorway. "Cassandra, I hope this time you give it a serious try and really get cured."

That was the dumbest thing to say. I kissed my mom quickly and hurried out before Aunt Dorothy's words could set her off again.

The picnic was on the river. There were no guys around, but I didn't care. My neck and shoulders hurt. Strange, but every time my mom gets upset, my neck hurts afterward. I chewed slowly on my roast beef sandwich while I watched Sarah and Uncle Tom skipping stones across the water. When Sarah's rock skipped three times, her dad lifted her up and swung her around. He didn't seem to mind that she was ugly.

That night my neck hurt so bad I hardly slept. And

when I did, I had icky nightmares. I felt crabby in the morning, and while Brenda and Kim were still arguing with Aunt Dorothy about being allowed to go to Seattle on the bus, I just took off. I didn't need them along, anyway.

Nanette wasn't busy, so she did my hair. She didn't say anything about my being alone. She just asked me about school's starting as she took strands of hair up between her fingers and clipped them off. After she was finished, she gave me a mirror and twirled my chair around so I could see the back of my head. My freshly shampooed hair gleamed like a smooth cap pulled over my head and down to the tips of my ears.

When I got back to their house, Sarah and her mom didn't say anything about my haircut. Brenda said it looked neat. Kim only nodded in agreement, but the next morning when we came down to breakfast, she checked me out carefully. I was wearing ice-washed jeans, a navy tank top, and a blue-striped shirt—with my antique-gold-colored earrings. I knew I looked cool, and I could tell it didn't make Kim particularly happy.

I wasn't particularly happy to be stuck walking to school with Brenda. As soon as we got inside the building, the teachers herded us into an assembly, and I managed to lose her. The top of the bleachers looked like where I wanted to be. I climbed up over yelling kids and took a seat next to a cute guy in a track sweatshirt.

Down below, a man I figured must be the vice-principal tapped on the microphone while a couple of boys scooted the cord between the chairs set up for the teachers. As the teachers gradually sat down, the kids started a one, two, three rhythm. Stamp, stamp, clap. Stamp, stamp, clap. Stamp, stamp, clap. I was just getting into it when they started "the wave."

I stared at the bleachers across the gym floor, where, one after the other, the kids slowly stood and then slowly sat down, creating waves along the benches. On our side of the gym, when it came my turn to stand, the guy beside me pulled me up by my hand. I shrugged my shoulders helplessly at him, and he laughed and took my hand again when it was time to sit down.

The vice-principal below was saying into the mike, "May I have your attention? May I have your attention? Let's quiet down now. Please quiet down. I know you're all anxious to get this assembly over so you can start work in your classes." That got a laugh.

He went on about how happy he and the teachers were to be back. Then he introduced the teachers and had them stand and tell what subject they taught. After that, the presidents of the boys' and girls' clubs stood up to address the student body and encourage each and every one to participate in their student government. The usual boring first-day stuff.

"So you must be new here," the guy beside me said.

"Ya." I nodded. "I'm from Seattle."

"Your family move to Marysville this summer?"

"No, my mom's sick, so I'm staying with my cousins until she's back home."

"Who're your cousins?"

"Kim Saxton?" I was noticing he had broad shoulders and a dimple in his chin.

"I think I know her. She's kinda cute with black hair. . . ." He bounced his fingers on top of his head, indicating Kim's mane.

"That's her," I said.

The vice-principal was giving orders for dismissal. All the students with class schedules were to go to their homerooms. All unregistered students were to remain seated. "That's me," I said.

He got up to hop down the bleachers. When he was one bench down, he turned. "What's your name?"

"Copper Jones. What's yours?"

"Ricky Layton." He hopped backward down another bench. "See ya, Copper." And he was gone in the crowd.

It took forever to get my report card evaluated and get a class schedule and then find the right wing and check all the numbers on the doors until I came to my homeroom. The teacher was the type who went over every item on the schedule I handed to her. She gave me a stern look. "I need your given name."

"It's Copper Jones."

"Not your nickname. I want your birth name."

"It's Copper. Copper." I pulled a strand of my hair out from my head. "See? Just like my hair."

The kids in the class laughed. And the one who laughed loudest was Ricky Layton.

Chapter
6

I'D EATEN LUNCH WITH BRENDA ON THAT FIRST DAY OF school. I didn't think it was necessary to walk home with her, too. But as soon as I got in the house, Aunt Dorothy asked me where Brenda was.

"She's probably coming along," I said. "One of the kids gave me a lift on a bike, so I got here faster."

It was twenty-five more minutes before Brenda showed up. When she came in the living room and saw me, she put her hands on her hips and demanded, "Where were you? I've been waiting and waiting and waiting for you. The janitor finally told me to go home."

"I got a ride on a bike," I said.

"You didn't even tell Brenda you were leaving?" my aunt asked.

"Well, the sixth grade wing is way over on the other side of the school," I explained. "And she never told me anything about meeting her."

"I walked way over to your side," Brenda said in a hurt voice.

Kim was slouched in her dad's big chair, lazily flipping through her mom's *Good Housekeeping*. I didn't think she'd been paying any attention until she looked up at me and asked, "Whose bike was it?"

"Um . . . Ricky Layton's," I said. "He's just a kid in my class."

"Sure, sure." A slow smile spread over her face as she looked back down at her magazine. "I know his brother."

Sarah bounced on the davenport. "I'm hungry. Can we have cookies or something until Dad gets home?"

"He isn't coming home for dinner tonight. He has a union meeting," Aunt Dorothy said. "But you can get some graham crackers out of the cupboard if you want."

While we were munching down, Aunt Dorothy reminded Kim and Brenda that they'd have to get an early dismissal the next day because they had a two o'clock dentist appointment. She turned to me. "Do you suppose you can remember to come right home from school and be with Sarah until we get back from the dentist's?"

"Sure," I said.

"Then I'll give you the house key in the morning."

"Why can't I have it?" Sarah whined.

"Because you lost it the last time," Kim told her.

Ricky met me outside the door of my sixth-period class. "Wanna ride home?" he asked.

"Sure," I said.

We wobbled out of the school yard, me on the seat, Ricky pumping in front. When we got to the street, he went all out, and we zipped along the roads beside the cars. The damp, cold wind was whooshing through my hair. I held on to Ricky's thin, hard waist and laughed.

It started to rain before we were halfway home. The bike tires slipped on the wet pavement, and we went down, barely escaping the wheels of a passing car.

Ricky pulled me up first and then his bike. "You all right?" he asked.

I brushed slimy leaves off my jeans. "I think so," I said.

Ricky thumped the bike up the curb, got down on his knees to check the spokes, and then wheeled the bike off the parking strip and down the sidewalk. I limped along beside him. "You did get hurt," he said.

"No, I think I just bruised a muscle when we crashed." I didn't want to say it was my bottom that was sore.

The rain came down harder. Ricky's brown hair flattened against his head. I felt mine stick to my ears as the water dripped onto my neck. There was a covered bus stop ahead of us. Ricky suggested we park there until the rain eased up.

I sat on the wooden bench with him, shivering in my wet clothes. "Get closer," he said, "and we'll get warm together."

I moved an inch toward him. I was too self-conscious to come any nearer. He bent his head and looked into my face. "What color are your eyes, anyway?"

"They're dark amber," I told him.

"They slant up a little on the ends. Like a wolf's."

" 'The better to see you, my dear,' " I said in a deep wolf voice.

After he laughed, there was silence between us. I

couldn't think of anything else to talk about. We sat there, looking at the rain pour off the roof of the bus shed. I was relieved when one of his friends rode up on his bike. Ricky and his friend, Chuck, clowned around awhile.

When Chuck left, Ricky turned to me again. "Do you like to go skating?"

"Roller skating?"

"Ya, there's a rink in town. My brother and I go most Friday nights. Why don't you go tomorrow night and bring your cousin Kim?"

"I don't know if my aunt will let us."

"Ah, you can work it out," he said.

I figured I could.

It wasn't until we were in sight of my aunt's house that I remembered Sarah. There she was, huddled against the front door, crying. I hurried on ahead of Ricky. "I'm sorry I'm late," I called out to her, "but we had an accident."

She kept on blubbering as I said a hurried good-bye to Ricky and rushed up the stairs to the porch. "We'll be all right," I assured her, "just as soon as we get inside and get warm." I tried to pat her shoulder, but she shrank away from me.

"No, I won't be all right! I'm freezing, and you're going to get it, Copper Jones." She looked out to the street. "And here comes Mom now."

I kept my back to the sound of the approaching car as I frantically searched in my pockets for the key. "Don't tell your mom. Don't tell her I was late. Just tell her we were playing in the yard, OK?" My hand was shaking so, I couldn't get the key upright in the lock.

There were footsteps on the stairs behind me. And then the feel of Aunt Dorothy yanking on my arm. "Give me the key," she ordered. "Did you just get home?"

"Yes, she did." Sarah's sobbing got louder. "She left me in the pouring rain for hours and hours."

"For one half hour. And I got wet, too. And hurt. We had an accident," I said to Aunt Dorothy as I followed her through the door.

When we all were inside, she faced me with a stern look. "What did you have the accident in?"

"On a . . . on a bike. It slipped in the street because of the rain."

"Ricky Layton, again," Kim put in knowingly.

Aunt Dorothy's expression turned to disgust. "You don't have any more sense of responsibility than your—" She closed her lips tight.

I knew what she was going to say. She was going to say I didn't have any more sense of responsibility than my mother. I watched my aunt Dorothy put her arm around Sarah and coo to her that she should have a nice, hot bath. I climbed the stairs to the bedroom alone.

There was nothing to do until dinner, so I lay on the bed with my Walkman on. Aunt Dorothy came in the room to get Sarah's dry clothes. She didn't speak to me. She never asked me if I was hurt. She just cared about her dense, ugly daughter, who could have waited in the garage and kept dry.

At dinner, my aunt was still tight-lipped. Uncle Tom did the talking, mostly about Uncle Raymond's campaign for state senator. I was keeping my head bent over my plate until he brought up the fund-raising dinner for Uncle Raymond that was supposed to be taking place the next night.

"But what will we do with the girls if we go?" Aunt Dorothy asked.

"We don't have to be there until seven," Uncle Tom said. "You can feed them first."

"And then drop us off at a show on your way. And pick us up on your way back." Kim sounded pleased with her idea.

"There you have it," Uncle Tom said to his wife.

It was Kim's and my turn to do the dishes. As soon as we were safely alone in the kitchen, I said, "Listen, Ricky and his brother want us to go skating tomorrow night."

Kim shook her head. "Mom will never go for it."

"Why not?"

"Because Friday night is when all the stoners show up. We can only go in the daytime."

I poured the liquid soap into the sink. I wanted to keep Kim in a good mood by letting her wipe the dishes. "There are plenty of stoners in Seattle. They never bothered me." I slipped the scraped plates into the hot water. "I know what we can do. We'll let Sarah and Brenda go into the theater first. We'll tell them I've seen the movie and we're going to the show on the other side of the building. And after they're inside, we'll split for the skating rink. And be back to meet them outside before your parents show up."

Kim, looking thoughtful, picked up the first rinsed plate. "How do you know Ricky's brother will come?"

"Because Ricky told me so. He said his brother asked for you. I guess he likes you." That was stretching it a bit, but it made her smile, and I smiled back.

Chapter
7

AUNT DOROTHY PRANCED INTO THE KITCHEN WHILE my cousins and I were eating dinner. She twirled twice around in her pink, beaded sweater dress. "Well, how do I look? Do you think I'll knock them dead at the fund-raiser?"

"You look pretty, Mom," Sarah said. "Your hair looks pretty."

"Been to the beauty parlor, huh?" Kim said between chews on the tough pizza crust.

Aunt Dorothy's hair did look better than usual. It was fluffed around her head instead of hanging down in lank, gray strings. The pink dress, however, might as well have been pulled over a tree trunk. Aunt Dorothy's as bulgy in front as she is in back.

I opened my mouth to ask her if there were any carrots in the refrigerator that I might have. I wanted some carrots or berries or oranges or something that wasn't doughy. She danced out of the kitchen before I could speak, though.

Kim studied the piece of pizza in her hand. "This thing stayed too long in the freezer."

"It does taste funny," Sarah agreed.

Brenda didn't say anything. She'd gobble up cat food.

Brenda and I cleaned up the kitchen together. I told her I'd washed last night, so it was her turn. She didn't object, probably because there weren't too many dishes. "How come Sarah never has to help?" I wanted to know.

"Because she's only eight."

"Only eight!" I snapped the towel in the air. "At eight, I was doing the dishes all by myself."

"Well," Brenda said, dumping two soapy cups into the rinse water, "Sarah is Mom's baby."

I fished out the cups and wiped them. "I don't remember ever being too little to clean up the house."

"What was it like being an only kid?"

"It was all right," I told her. "I was alone a lot. But then my mom let me have friends over whenever I wanted."

"That must have been neat," Brenda said.

Sometimes it was neat. As I wiped the dishes, I remembered a time it wasn't. I'd invited a girl called Carolyn over for the night. My mom was having a party, but it wasn't too wild of a party. Carolyn and I were climbing the stairs to go up to my room. Mom was in the hall below with some man. "Wooo, wooo, wooo," she sang with her face tilted up to his. "Wooo, wooo, wooo, I'm a night owl."

I didn't think that was too bad, but when we got into my room, Carolyn said she wanted to go home.

"Why?" I asked her.

"I just want to," she said.

"But why?"

"Everybody's drinking."

"They won't bother us," I assured her. "Come on. Let's play some darts."

But she wouldn't and she insisted that she wanted to go home and she did. I was embarrassed. I didn't invite anyone over to stay the night for quite a long time after that.

When Brenda and I finished the dishes, I went upstairs to change my clothes. Sarah was on her bed with my Walkman beside her and the earphones on her head. I snatched them off and gave her hair a good pull at the same time. "You leave my things alone, rat mouth."

She beetled downstairs, yowling for her mother.

I shouldn't have done that. It put Sarah in a whiny mood, and she gave Kim and me a hard time at the entrance to the theater. "I don't see why you can't go in with us," she complained. "Just because your movie is behind another door doesn't mean we can't get our tickets together."

Brenda was real quiet. I think she suspected something.

"I'll get our tickets," Kim said. "I'll get our tickets." When she came back from the cashier's window, she was holding up a closed fist. From it she pulled out one ticket for Brenda and another for Sarah. "Now," she said, giving Sarah a push toward the entrance, "we'll meet both of you right here when the movie's over."

Kim and I held our breath until her sisters disappeared

inside the theater door. "Aw right! Here we go!" I shouted. "You lead the way."

Ricky and his brother, Tim, were already in the skating rink when we got there. They zoomed up to us on their skates while we were lacing up ours. Ricky made the introductions.

"Kim, Tim. Tim, Kim." I laughed. "Great! You two rhyme."

As soon as I was on the floor, I dashed to the end of the rink, swirled around in circles with my feet stretched wide, and yelled, "I'm free! I'm free."

"Not anymore. I've caught you," Ricky yelled back, grabbing my waist with both his hands. He held on to me, pushing me forward while I skated fast and he skated faster. Round and around the rink we flew. I tapped Kim on the shoulder each time we passed her. "Out of the way. Out of the way," Ricky hollered at her and his brother.

The music stopped, leaving only the sound of wheels scraping on the floor in the big hall.

"Clear the rink. Everybody clear out of the middle of the rink for the limbo stick," the announcer said.

Ricky steered me to the side wall, where Kim and Tim joined us. I was out of breath and my chest was heaving up and down while we watched the attendants set the limbo stick on stands in the middle of the floor.

"All right now. Let's all of you go under the stick in a nice easy line," the announcer directed.

The four of us followed the crowd to the end of the room and then up to and under the limbo stick. We all made it the first and second times, but the third time the stick was lowered, Kim splatted onto the floor. I hooted with laughter. The fifth time under, I lost my balance and fell from my crouch and she hooted back at me. Ricky and Tim went down the sixth time under.

"I'm thirsty," Ricky said when he and his brother met us at the sidelines. They had money for pop, so we all skated over to the food stands, got four Pepsis, and took them to a table.

Kim looked at her watch, then looked at me. "We got ten minutes before we have to split."

The movie wasn't out yet when Kim and I arrived at the theater, which made me glad. I didn't want any more trouble with Aunt Dorothy. But when the movies did let out and all the people streamed by us, there was no Sarah or Brenda.

"The dummies are probably inside looking for us," Kim said. "I'll go get them." She talked the ticket-taker into letting her make a run into the theater while I stood outside. Unfortunately, that was just when Uncle Tom drove up.

Aunt Dorothy rolled down the car window. "Where are the others?"

"They're coming. They're coming," I said. "Kim and I went through another door and we must have missed Sarah and Brenda in the crowd."

I turned back toward the theater entrance just as the cousins came out. "You were *not* in the other movie," Sarah was saying, "because we got out first and we looked for you."

"Oh, you're blind," Kim told her.

We all climbed in the back of the car under Aunt Dorothy's suspicious gaze. As her dad pulled out into the traffic, Kim leaned forward against his seat. "You would have loved the movie we saw, Dad. It was about this big sailing ship that makes a trip to the North Pole and—"

"Ya, and you would have liked ours, too," Sarah interrupted. "It was about these kids who found a treasure map and were following the directions to find the gold when these three mean men . . ."

She prattled on with the whole plot while I leaned back. I figured Kim had us home free until we got in the house and Aunt Dorothy took Sarah by the arm and said, "You girls go on up to your rooms. I want to talk to Sarah down here."

Yuck. I followed Kim and Brenda slowly up the stairs, dragging my stomach behind me. Ten minutes later, Aunt Dorothy called us back down to the living room. Brenda and I entered hesitantly. Kim sauntered ahead of us. "Whatever it is, I didn't do it."

Uncle Tom was leaning forward a bit in his big chair. He watched us with such a sad, concerned expression that I wanted to run. But Aunt Dorothy frightened me worse when she ordered the three of us to sit down on the davenport. We sat there, lined up like three scared birds, while she pinned us with a grim stare.

She started in on Brenda first. "Brenda, did Kim and Copper go into the movie theater with you?"

"I think so," Brenda said. "Kim bought the tickets."

"Did you see them go into the theater?"

"Well, Sarah and I went in first, so they were behind us."

"Did you see them after your show was out?"

I could feel a shiver go through Brenda as she swallowed before she answered her mother. For the first time, I liked Brenda. "A . . . well, we looked for them," she began, "but there were so many people, we just sort of hung around by the popcorn stand. And then Kim found us."

Aunt Dorothy stood over Brenda, eyeing her closely. "Go on upstairs," she finally told her. "And go to bed."

While Brenda hurried out of the room, I took in a slow breath and watched Aunt Dorothy move to the chair across the room and sit down. Was it over? Kim shifted beside me. "Well, now what?" she asked in a nasty voice.

"Now we'll just sit here until you're ready to tell your dad and me where you went this evening."

Kim opened her mouth to speak.

"And don't give me any lies," Aunt Dorothy added coldly. "I know you didn't see the movie."

Kim closed her mouth.

We sat. And sat. And sat. I tried to keep my gaze on the lamp table between my aunt and uncle, but when I felt Uncle Tom looking at me, I stared at the floor. Kim sighed, stretched, curled her legs under her, and leaned her head on the pillows. I waited, my shoulders getting stiffer and stiffer.

"Well, Kim?" Aunt Dorothy said.

Kim threw up her hands. "You let us off. You picked us up. What could we do?"

"You tell me," her mother said.

Kim sighed again.

Aunt Dorothy looked at her husband, then back at Kim. "All right," she said. "If this is the way you want it to be, you'll come home every day after school and go to your room. No radio, no TV, no phone, and you may come out of your room only to eat and go to the bathroom. There will be no exceptions. Not for your birthday, not for a school function, not for anything. Right, Tom?"

Uncle Tom nodded.

Kim got up from the davenport and started out of the room. I rose uncertainly after her. If I said anything, I'd get her in trouble. If I didn't say anything, I'd keep her on restriction. At the doorway she wheeled around. "OK, OK, we walked over to the skating rink. It wasn't any big deal."

Aunt Dorothy's face froze. "Whose idea was that?"

Kim didn't reply. For the first time that evening, Aunt Dorothy turned to me. "It was my idea," I said.

"I thought so." She wrinkled her nose as if she were smelling rotten meat.

"Go on to bed, now. Both of you," Uncle Tom told us. "We'll talk about this again in the morning."

At the top of the stairs, Kim said, "If you have any more bright ideas, Copper, don't include me." She went in her room and slammed her door.

Sarah had the light still on in our room. I didn't look

at her when I walked past her bed. I ignored her while I took off my clothes and put on my pajamas. I felt her watching me silently until I pulled the cover back from the pillow. "Copper, you did something to that quilt and I could tell Mom about that, too."

I looked up at her then and snarled, "Go ahead, you horse-toothed turd."

She stared back at me, her eyes widening, her mouth pursing into a tight circle. "I will!" She jumped out of bed, grabbed her robe, and tore out of the room.

Knowing I'd made things ten times worse, I sank down on the mattress and waited fearfully for her to return. She didn't. Not the whole night.

Chapter
8

ABOUT NINE O'CLOCK IN THE MORNING, AUNT DOROTHY came into the room, bent over my bed, and carefully examined the quilt. In the night I'd tried to pull the matted insides apart, but it hadn't worked very well.

"You come down to breakfast and then right back up here," she said coldly. "We're making some other plans for you."

Sarah was the only one left at the breakfast table. She smirked into my face as she passed me the box of Rice Krispies. I ate the cereal silently.

Alone in the bedroom, I felt the day pass slowly. All of my rock magazines were old. I got sick of music, and my ears itched from the fuzzy earphones.

There was only one chair in the dinky room. A wooden, yellow one, which matched the dresser and the walls. I sat in it for a while, lay on the bed, sat in the chair, then stared out of the window. It was strange being Copper. Why was I Copper? Why not Kim?

They let me come downstairs for dinner, but nobody

spoke to me. Nobody spoke to Kim, either, so I guessed she was on restriction, too. Once, from across the dining room table, I caught a small, sympathetic glance from Brenda. I attempted a small, wavering smile in return.

After dinner, I slept awhile. When I awoke, it was dark outside. I got up to go to the bathroom, and on my way back to the bedroom I heard soft voices from the living room topped by the big, booming voice of Uncle Raymond. I crept along the hall to the stairs, padded down three steps, and sat close to the banister where I thought I wouldn't be seen.

"That doesn't mean a thing," Uncle Raymond was saying. "She thinks she's losing a meal ticket, so she gets herself dried out. That kid's her responsibility. Not that Cassandra's ever taken responsibility for anything."

"Papa spoiled Cassandra." That was Aunt Judith's voice.

"What about the kid's father?" Uncle Raymond asked. "Didn't he have a sister?"

"Yes, but I don't think Cassandra would want Copper with her," Aunt Dorothy said. "She's into witchcraft."

Uncle Raymond's laugh rumbled up the stairs. "It sounds to me like they'd suit each other fine."

"Copper's just twelve years old," Uncle Tom said. He was the only one who cared about me, it seemed. I leaned my head against the banister.

"Well"—Aunt Dorothy's voice took on a firm note—"I can't have Copper here influencing my girls. And I can't make Sarah suffer any longer."

I jerked my head up straight. Sarah suffer! Talk about spoiled!

"Let me get you some more coffee. How about you, Judith?" That was Aunt Dorothy's voice again, and it was coming nearer.

I scrambled up the stairs, down the hall, and swiftly through my door. After I was in my bed, I wished I'd stayed around the corner in the upper hall. What were they saying in the living room? Aunt Dorothy would get rid of me for sure. But to where?

I flopped this way and that most of the night. I wished I could call my mother, but in my heart I knew she wouldn't be much help. What can you do when you're twelve? I couldn't even think of a place to run to.

In the morning, I pulled myself out of the tangled bed sheets. My eyes were burning and my head aching. I went to the bathroom, dressed, and then sat on the yellow, wooden chair to wait for the verdict.

Aunt Dorothy came in at nine-thirty. She sat primly down on Sarah's bed, oozing self-righteousness. I knew what was coming. A lecture.

"Now, Copper," she began, "when we took you in, we really thought you would enjoy the girls and they would enjoy you. But it didn't work out that way, did it?"

I wasn't about to answer her.

"Sarah's only eight years old," she explained, "and I can't have her hysterical every other day because you've called her a nasty name. She'll grow up to her teeth in time, but right now it isn't kind to make fun of them, is it?"

I still didn't answer.

The sides of my aunt's mouth were beginning to turn down in exasperation, but she went determinedly on. "When you are visiting in someone else's house, Copper, it is only courteous and considerate to follow the rules. Otherwise, you may find out that you're not welcome. That's a hard lesson for you to learn at your age, but I hope this time you've learned it.

"Now, your aunt Judith and uncle Raymond have agreed to take you until your mother's well. Raymond isn't as easygoing as Tom, so I think you'd be wise to do your very best to get along." She stood and brushed imaginary wrinkles from the front of her dress. "They'll be here to pick you up right after church. I'm sorry, but you'd better get your things packed."

Didn't I get to eat?

"Oh." She stopped at the door. "You might want your breakfast before you start packing."

The kitchen was empty when I entered. There was only one place set at the table. No one came in while I ate my bowl of cold cereal. I tried not to think of Jeff's Sunday breakfasts. I tried not to cry.

When I was half finished folding my clothes, Aunt Dorothy called me to come downstairs. I barely got to the living room before she herded me back into the kitchen. "Your mother's on the phone," she said. "You can talk to her in here."

I picked up the wall phone by the counter.

"Copper," Mom said, "what is going on?"

"I'm getting kicked out."

"So Dorothy told me. But why?"

"Because I hand-washed, in cold water, a quilt that stunk."

"But I don't understand," my mother said. "Why didn't you ask Dorothy to have it dry-cleaned? She said you ruined it."

"I did ask her. She wouldn't do it."

"What else happened?"

"I went to a skating rink for an hour instead of going to a movie. And when Sarah narked on Kim and me, I called her a name."

"What was wrong with the skating rink?"

"Nothing."

There was silence on the line. I wondered if my mom was still there. Then I heard her take a big breath. "Well, Dorothy always was a prig. Listen, darling, try to be nice at Judith's, OK?"

"Uncle Raymond doesn't want me," I told her.

"Oh, you can get along with him," she assured me. "Flatter him a little. He loves it. And you've always liked Judith, haven't you?"

"Yes," I said, "but does she like me?"

"*I* love you."

My chest heaved; tears I didn't want flooded my eyes. I reached in my jeans pocket for a tissue, but there wasn't one. "Mom," I said, "that isn't much help right now."

"I know, honey, but it's just a few more weeks. You're a smart girl. Just do what Judith and Raymond tell you. And, Copper-baby, I miss you."

"I miss you, too," I said, and hung up the phone, wiped my eyes with the sleeve of my shirt, and went upstairs to finish my packing.

Brenda slipped in the door after I had my jacket on and was settled in the yellow chair with the filled boxes at my feet. She held a Mars bar out to me. "Here," she said. "I bet you didn't have much to eat."

"Thanks," I said.

"Umm. I guess my mom is a lot stricter than your mom."

I nodded.

"Anyway, I'm . . . I'm sorry for what happened. I hope you have a good time at Aunt Judith's."

I nodded again.

" 'Bye," she said and slipped back out the door.

I sat for another half hour on the yellow chair, waiting, and wiping my eyes on my jacket sleeve.

Chapter
9

"WELL, HOW DO YOU LIKE YOUR NEW ROOM?" AUNT
Judith stood with her arm around my shoulders while
Uncle Raymond walked past us and deposited my boxes
by the closet.

"It's gorgeous," I said. "I'll feel like a princess in here.
I bet I'll even be able to feel a pea under the mattress."

"What!" Uncle Raymond stood up from the boxes and
looked at me in alarm.

Aunt Judith laughed. "The princess. The real princess
in the fairy tale could feel a pea under a pile of mattresses."

"Oh." Uncle Raymond hurried out of the room.

"Don't mind him," Aunt Judith told me. "I don't think
he ever was a child."

I stroked the folds of the gold and white satiny cloth
that hung down to the bed. "This canopy! I've never seen
a canopy outside of a picture book."

"I know," Aunt Judith said. "That's how I wanted this
room. Like a picture book."

"But my boxes look gross in here." Especially, I

thought, with that plastic hard hat sticking out. "I'll empty them and hide them away."

"I'll help you." She followed me to the closet and opened the lid of the first carton. "You don't own any suitcases?"

"Mom took all of hers to the center, and Jeff took all of his, and all I own is this tote bag. I never needed anything else before." Saying that made me feel sad inside—like an orphan. I hoped desperately that I'd get along here, but I didn't know how to tell that to Aunt Judith.

After she left with the empty cartons, I wandered over the Chinese rug, touching the lace-edged pillow cases on the canopy bed, the backs of the soft gold chairs, and the dark wood of the carved writing desk. I'd be afraid to stack my school books on the desk. School! I'd have to face another new school. Without Brenda this time. Poor Brenda, stuck with that narky little sister.

Aunt Judith came back into the bedroom dangling a blue swimsuit from one hand. "How would you like to go swimming?" she asked.

"Great. But where? Will that fit me?"

"I think so. It has adjustable straps." She held the suit out to me. "Try it on. Our condo has a pool."

I didn't fill out the suit in front as much as Aunt Judith would, but since it was tank style it looked OK. Luckily, Aunt Judith weighed about fifty pounds less than Aunt Dorothy.

We went down to the pool without Uncle Raymond. He

was busy writing a speech for a banquet. The pool was big, the water was warm, and there were two cute guys there who managed to "accidentally" splash me. Kim would have loved it.

Aunt Judith said she and I would go out to dinner together because Uncle Raymond was meeting with two of his advisers. She took me to Bruseau's in downtown Edmonds. Edmonds has old-fashioned buildings and hanging flower baskets along the streets, and it ends in a ferry dock on Puget Sound.

It was a warm fall day, so Aunt Judith and I carried our dinner trays out to the wooden tables in front of the restaurant. I had quiche Lorraine and a green salad and mint tea and poppy seed–lemon cake. "This is delicious. This is wonderful," I told Aunt Judith. And then I said more softly as I sipped my tea, "You know, I didn't really mean to be bad at Aunt Dorothy's."

The umbrella above the table slanted shade across Aunt Judith's face. Her brown eyes took on a soft glow. "I know you didn't. Don't worry about it. We'll have fun together."

I was sure we would.

But I didn't have much fun the next day at school. It was a regular junior high, and seventh graders were nothings. I got lost three times before lunch. At lunch I didn't know which line to get in; I didn't know where to sit. Finally, I just got a hamburger and milk and sat down in the nearest empty space.

The two girls across from me looked up from their

private conversation. "You're new here, aren't you," one said.

There was a catch in her question somewhere. "What's the matter? Am I at the wrong table?"

"No," she answered. "You can sit anyplace, but you're eating a hamburger."

"So?" I stared down at my bun.

"It's made of soybeans," the second girl told me.

I'd wondered why it tasted so dry. The girls went back to discussing the guys in their classes and didn't talk to me again.

I dumped my milk carton and the last third of my bun in the garbage can and went out of the cafeteria to wander around the halls. That got old fast. There were only a few halls the kids could be in at lunchtime, and I felt stupid walking up and down them by myself.

I went in the girls' john and combed and combed my already smooth hair and then hid in a stall while groups of girls came in and out, laughing and joking with one another. The bell ending lunchtime was a relief. My fifth-period social studies class was as dry as the school soybean burgers, but sitting in there beat sitting on a toilet.

We had Dungeness crab for dinner that night. Uncle Raymond cleaned the crabs, cracked them, and spread them out on a platter of ice. Aunt Judith made a salad of avocado and grapefruit slices. "This looks like your campaign banquet," I said as I sat down at the table.

Uncle Raymond seemed pleased. I remembered Mom said he liked flattery, and I was doing my best. When we'd eaten the last crab leg, Uncle Raymond said to me, "We made the dinner. How about you doing the dishes?"

"I'd be glad to." I popped up from my place and began clearing the table.

He followed me into the kitchen to show me where the dishwasher soap was, and the sink cleaner. "We don't have a disposal, so you have to take the garbage out to the cans in the back of the building."

"Fine," I said.

It didn't take me long to get the dishwasher filled and the counters shining. There were only crab shells, peelings, and paper napkins in the sack under the sink. I figured I'd empty the sack in the morning. It would be light out then.

Uncle Raymond came in to check how I'd done. "It looks very nice," he said.

"Thank you," I said.

"Did you get the garbage?"

"No, there's just a little bit. I'll do it after breakfast. Before I go to school," I assured him.

"I'd rather you did it now."

"But the sack isn't even half full." I explained. "There will be more in the morning."

"Crab can smell up this whole kitchen by tomorrow morning."

"But they're only shells. They'll be . . ." The muscles twitching along his jaw stopped me. A warning shiver was going down my arms. I opened the cupboard beneath the sink, snatched out the sack, and dashed from the kitchen saying, "You're right. Crab shells can stink. I don't know what I was thinking. . . ."

It was coal-black outside the building where the garbage cans sat. I took a big breath at the door, zipped out to the cans, dumped the sack in, and zipped back in the door. I stood a minute at the bottom of the stairs, holding on to the metal railing. I didn't know if I was breathing hard because I was scared of the dark or because of my argument with Uncle Raymond. Don't argue with him, stupid, I told myself.

The next morning, I was carefully sweet. I popped up again from the table when we had finished breakfast, cleared off the dishes, cleaned the kitchen, and took the garbage out. Uncle Raymond didn't compliment me, but his jaw muscles weren't twitching while he checked the counters and the cupboard beneath the sink.

School was the same trip. At noon I got in the hot-lunch line and had a better meal, but still nobody talked to me. And I had nothing to do but wander around by myself and hide in the john stall until the fifth-period bell rang. I was relieved to get back to the condo.

This night was Uncle Raymond's banquet. Aunt Judith had asked the lady next door to come in and keep me company because she and my uncle would be getting home late in the night. Just when they were dressed and ready to go out the door, the lady called and said she felt the flu coming on.

"I'm so sorry," Aunt Judith said into the phone. "Don't worry about us. Just get into bed and keep warm."

After she hung up, she said to Uncle Raymond, "I guess I'll have to stay here with Copper."

I had come in from the kitchen where I was making myself a toasted cheese sandwich. "Oh, no. I can stay by myself. My mom never got me a baby-sitter." I could tell by Uncle Raymond's expression that that hadn't been exactly the right thing to say.

He turned to his wife. "Isn't there someone else you can ask to come in? I'd like you to go with me. How about Dorothy?"

"I don't think so," Aunt Judith said.

I didn't think so, either. "It's all right, really. I'm twelve, and I can just watch TV awhile and then go to bed."

"Maybe she'll be all right alone," Aunt Judith suggested.

Uncle Raymond looked at his watch. "Well . . ." Then he looked sternly at me. "You double-lock the front door, don't answer the phone, and be in bed by ten."

"I will. I will."

"Are you sure?" he asked.

"I'm sure. I'll be fine."

Aunt Judith kissed me good-bye, and they went off to their banquet.

I had lied about being fine by myself. Ever since I was a little kid, I've been afraid of being in the house alone at night. My mom would always say gaily, "Oh, Copper doesn't mind," and trot off to her parties, leaving me shivering at the window.

After my aunt and uncle left, I checked under all the beds and in the closets, and put the chain on the kitchen door before I sat down with my sandwich to watch TV. Even then I cringed when I heard footsteps in the outside hall. At ten sharp, I got ready for bed. It took me a long time to go to sleep. I don't really remember when I drifted off.

Chapter
10

SCR-RATCH. I OPENED MY EYES. WHAT WAS THAT?
Maybe my uncle putting his key in the lock. Scraping,
scraping sounds. Maybe he was drunk and couldn't find
the lock.

I listened, barely breathing. If my uncle was drunk, my
aunt would take the key from him, wouldn't she?

Doorknob turning. Silence. Scraping. Doorknob clicking. Silence. Scraping. I slid my hand up to my neck and
felt the swallow lift and drop in my throat. Somebody,
somebody was trying to get in.

My eyes stared through the dark at the ceiling. Scraping. Clicking. Clicking. I held myself rigid, frozen like a
rabbit in headlights.

The dead bolt. Did I turn the dead bolt in the door
before I went to bed? I had switched off the TV with the
remote control, crumpled my napkin onto my sandwich
plate, got up and turned off the living room light. . . .
Before the light, did I check the door? Did I turn the dead
bolt? Did I switch the hall light on and then check the
door?

Scraping again. Clicking. It has to be a burglar. He must be trying the knob so much because he's got one lock open, but he hasn't got the dead bolt yet. Please, please let the dead bolt hold, I prayed.

Clicking. Clicking. Do something, you dense idiot, I told myself. Get out of bed. Go look. Go see before you're caught like a rabbit.

I slithered out of my bed as quietly as possible, softly opened my bedroom door, and crept down the hall. At the entrance to the living room, I stopped. Across the room a crack of light shone around the edge of the front door. He had a flashlight.

I couldn't see the doorknob turn, but I could hear it. My breath halted as I waited to see if the door would open. It didn't.

The phone. I was so scared I could only repeat in my head, the phone, the phone! I made myself move, made myself feel around the big leather chair and inch toward the coffee table. I stopped again. He would hear me call here, but not in Aunt Judith's room.

I crept back down the hall, my legs shaking so they could hardly hold me up. I found Aunt Judith's door and fumbled my way along the bed. I didn't want a light on. I didn't want a light on because if he got in the house, he could see where I was.

The phone clunked on the stand when my hand hit it. I felt along the row of buttons until I came to the last one. I heard it ring, ring again. Hurry. Please, please hurry, I begged.

"Operator."

"Someone's trying to get in the door," I told her in a rush. "I'm all alone. Get the police, quick. It's the Lake-Shore condominiums. Number 7—"

She interrupted me. "I'll connect you with the police department."

Hurry. Please, hurry.

The front door squeaked open.

I hung up the phone, crouched to my knees, and slipped under the bed.

Steps. Light steps. Another squeaky sound. The VCR pulled off the TV?

Steps nearer. Steps away. Distant shuffling.

I pinched my nose closed to stop a sneeze. Sloppy house-cleaning lady. As I breathed through my mouth, the dust came down my throat. I pressed both hands hard over my face, and the sneeze exploded in my fingers.

I listened, my thighs trembling against the cold, bare floor. Distant shuffling. Not nearer. Then nearer!

Panic gripped me and froze me still.

A light switching back and forth on the floor beside me. Drawers opening. Hinge creaking. Aunt Judith's jewel case. Take them, I pleaded silently. Take the jewels and leave.

Steps coming closer. Terrified, I watched the comforter slip to the floor, heard the mattress yanked in the air. I clamped my teeth into my cheeks to keep from screaming. Oh, God. Oh, please, no! Oh, please don't let him see me.

A siren!

Mattress thumping back down. Steps toward window. Be scared away. Please be scared away.

I listened to the siren winding down, my thighs trembling again.

Steps going toward the dresser. Quick steps away, down the hall. Front door closing. He was gone!

My mouth opened, and my chest heaved in gulps of dusty air. Tears of relief slipped down my cheeks as the sound of shouting and scuffling came from the outside halls. My breath slowed and my mouth closed. The hollow echo of deep voices came through car speakers.

The front door opened. "Police!"

I didn't move.

"Maybe she got out before he came in."

"Let's check the back rooms."

I slid out from under the bed.

In the living room, the biggest cop complimented me on my fast thinking. "It's better if you can leave the premises, but if you can't, calling the police and hiding is the next best thing."

"Some people freeze like sitting ducks," the smaller policeman said.

Or rabbits, I thought, but didn't say so.

"Here, you're shaking." The big policeman took Aunt Judith's afghan off the davenport and threw it around my shoulders. "Sit down a minute. Now, what I'm wondering is how come a young girl like you is left alone in an apartment at one o'clock in the morning?"

"Well," I began, "my . . . my mother's having a treatment, and while she's having it, I'm staying with my aunt and uncle."

Both policemen had seated themselves on the davenport. The big one looked at me expectantly as if he was waiting for me to finish.

I shifted in the leather chair. "A . . . my aunt and uncle were going to a party, and only grown-ups were invited, so I stayed here. Alone. It's . . . it's OK."

"How long will your mother be having her 'treatment'?" the little cop asked. He was writing things down on a clipboard.

"A month or a month and a half altogether, I guess." I glanced up. Aunt Judith and Uncle Raymond were coming through the front door.

Aunt Judith looked alarmed. Uncle Raymond looked stern. He nodded toward the police. "What's been happening here?"

Both policemen got to their feet. The big one told my uncle about my phone call and how they caught the robber running down the outside hall. "We have some jewelry here." The big cop pulled a plastic bag from his pocket and took out Aunt Judith's string of pearls and pearl ring.

"Those are mine," she said.

"We figured they might be." He stuffed the pearls back in the bag. "We'll have to hold them temporarily for evidence."

Aunt Judith nodded and then came to sit on the arm of my chair. "Are you all right?" she asked me.

Before I could answer, the big cop said, "We're a little concerned about her. We don't like to see children left alone at one o'clock in the morning."

"She wasn't harmed?" my uncle said.

"No," the cop answered, "she had the good sense to hide. But I don't believe any of us want to think about what might have happened if he'd found her."

A chill ran down my back, and Aunt Judith put her arm around me.

"We had a previous commitment we didn't feel we could ignore," my uncle explained in his smooth lawyer manner. "Our niece has just been left with us for a few days."

A few days! My uncle caught me wrinkling my nose. "Go put a robe on," he ordered.

I looked down at my nipples poking out the thin material of my pajama top, felt my face go hot, and hurried out of the room.

Chapter
11

IN THE MORNING, I AWOKE WITH A THROBBING HEAD-
ache. I lay in bed remembering the burglary. With the
morning sunlight streaming through the curtains, it
seemed as if it had been a nightmare, that it couldn't have
happened.

I eased out of bed, got dressed, and went to the bathroom. On the way to the dining room, I stopped. My aunt
and uncle were talking about me.

My uncle was saying he simply couldn't afford an investigation. Maybe there won't be one, Aunt Judith said
back. "Some newspaper will be sure to check the officers'
shift report," Uncle Raymond replied, "and you can bet
that will bring a reporter around, sniffing for a child-
neglect case."

"Well then, what do you want me to do?" my aunt
asked.

"My schedule is full this morning. You get her settled
and come on in later."

Aunt Judith worked in Uncle Raymond's office, so it

would be all right for her to be late. But what did they mean about getting me settled?

"What if Dorothy won't take her back?" my aunt asked.

Dorothy! Aunt Dorothy? I put both of my hands around my neck and held it tight.

"Then take her over to her father's sister." My uncle was getting impatient, I could tell by his voice.

"Cassandra never thought Margo was a stable person," Aunt Judith said softly. I guess she knew he was impatient, too.

"What would Cassandra know about stability?" he asked. "Does this Margo work?"

"Yes, I think she's a manager at Boeing."

"A manager? That doesn't sound like the type that shoves little children in an oven. . . ."

I took a big breath and hurried into the dining room. "I've got an idea. I've got an idea." I was thinking as fast as I could while my surprised aunt and uncle gaped at me. "This will work, I know." I sat down with them at the table. "You . . . you just call Aunt Dorothy and have her say she was supposed to come over and baby-sit me. And . . . and Uncle Tom would take care of her kids. But after you left for the banquet, Aunt Dorothy called me and said Sarah had the flu and she couldn't come. And so you never knew I was alone until you got home."

Uncle Raymond stared at me for a long minute. "You really think I'm going to explain all that on TV?"

"Or maybe you could say," I rushed on, "that Uncle

Tom took Brenda and Kim to a show, and Aunt Dorothy was going to bring Sarah with her over here, but when Sarah started throwing up, she couldn't bring her and she couldn't leave her home alone."

Uncle Raymond put his big hand on my shoulder. "Look, Copper, I know you didn't get along with Dorothy and you don't know your father's sister very well, but you're only going to stay with one of them for a few weeks. And I can't put myself in a position that will give my opponent ammunition to use against me. He's the incumbent and he's already ahead.

"If you really think about it, you'll understand that it doesn't make sense for me to risk losing a chance to be a state senator just so you can visit with us for three weeks. Right?"

"But . . . but the police already know I was alone last night." I looked up at Uncle Raymond, who was rising from his chair.

"We'll tell anyone interested that you were only visiting for a couple of days, which is true, and that you've gone to stay with another aunt until your mother is finished with her cure. That will end it here. After all, you're twelve years old. You might get some questions from a reporter afterward. Tell the truth. That the sitter we had planned for you called in ill. And that should wrap up the whole investigation." He patted my shoulder again, bent down and kissed Aunt Judith, picked up his briefcase, and left.

"How about your helping yourself to some scrambled

eggs and toast while I make some phone calls." Aunt Judith gave me an encouraging smile as she got up from her chair.

I put a hand out, trying to hold her with me. "I don't think Aunt Dorothy will ever have me back."

Aunt Judith hesitated, put her fingers over her mouth, and thought for a few seconds. "Well, maybe I should try your aunt Margo first."

"No, no." I got up and begged with both hands. "Mom thinks she's evil."

"Copper, your mother's prejudiced. She never wanted your father to pay attention to any woman except her."

"But Aunt Margo's a witch."

"If she is, you don't have to be prejudiced, too. And anyway, I'll meet Margo first and talk to her. You sit down and eat."

I sat down, but I didn't eat. Instead, I listened to the phone conversations in the living room. First, Aunt Judith called the operator and asked for the number of a Margo Jones who lived in either Everett or the Lake Stevens area. Second, she called Aunt Margo, introduced herself, and asked for a meeting as soon as it would be convenient.

She ended the conversation with, "Right. I'll be there in a half hour."

Aunt Judith didn't come back into the dining room. She went directly to her bedroom. Searching my mind frantically for a new idea, I got up from my chair.

"Aunt Judith," I said at her door, "couldn't I go to a

show this evening in case the reporters come. Then you could just tell them I'd left for good."

"No, Copper. It's very foolish to lie during a political campaign. If you're found out, it's disastrous." She was taking her coat off the hanger in the closet.

I moved close to her. "Aunt Judith, please, please. It isn't my fault. It was my fault at Aunt Dorothy's, but it isn't my fault here. It isn't fair."

She moved right by me to pick her purse up off the dresser. "I know it isn't fair, but it also isn't the end of the world."

"Aunt Judith." I planted myself right in front of her and looked up into her eyes. "What happens if Jeff doesn't take my mom back. How will we live?"

That stopped her, but only for a moment. "I don't have all the answers, Copper, but I don't think that's something for you to be worrying about."

That's something *you* don't have to worry about, I wanted to say. You're all safe in this pretty condominium. But I didn't say it.

"You eat your breakfast now. And when you're finished, get your things organized and ready to pack." She kissed me on the cheek and started for the living room. "Oh, wait a minute. You better come with me. Go get your jacket and a couple pieces of toast. No, wait, you get your jacket and I'll make you a scrambled egg sandwich to go, OK?"

OK? You just don't want to get yourself in more trouble, I thought. I got my jacket and waited for her at the front door. She held the sandwich out to me. I didn't take it. "I'm not hungry," I told her.

"Well, carry it, then. We've got to hurry."

I put the sandwich on the end table beside the davenport and followed her out the door. She didn't seem much like sweet Aunt Judith anymore. We didn't talk in the car. She just drove fast down the freeway, turned off the ramp, and parked in front of a restaurant called Victor's.

"You stay here," she said. "Margo only has time for a quick cup of coffee before she has to be at work."

"Some big meeting to see what the witch is like," I muttered. As I watched her walk toward the entrance of the building, I thought bitterly how I'd believed she was too nice for Uncle Raymond. And then she turned out just like him.

It wasn't fifteen minutes before Aunt Judith came out the restaurant door with another woman. It had been five years since I'd seen Aunt Margo, but I recognized her long, black hair that was held together at the back of her neck by a silver barrette. I took a real good look as she got in her car in the parking lot. Before she closed the car door, she turned and waved at me. I didn't wave back.

Aunt Judith got in our car. "Margo seems real nice," she said.

"I feel like one of those white elephant presents that people give away again as fast as possible."

"Copper, this all just happened." Aunt Judith drove out of the parking lot and headed for the freeway. "I'm sorry you feel bad, but nobody is to blame."

"Yes, but it's me that's getting given away." I let myself cry then—half because I wanted my aunt to know how bad I felt and half because I was scared.

Aunt Judith didn't seem to notice my tears until we pulled up in front of the junior high. "Here, honey, here's a tissue." She tried to hand it to me, but I just let it fall in my lap. "Copper, do you want to go in with me, or shall I just get your withdrawal papers myself?"

"You do it," I said. "It's your idea."

I sat in the car and waited and waited. I really didn't feel like crying anymore. I felt empty and hollow and dry inside. And hopeless. I leaned my head against the car window and tears slipped down my face anyway.

When Aunt Judith came back, I sat up slowly. She put the school papers on the dashboard before she started up the car. "That school seemed nice. The kids in the office were friendly."

"Maybe to you," I said.

"You don't like school?" she asked as she steered out onto the road.

"I liked mine in Seattle. I liked the one in Marysville."

She glanced over at me. "I can still try Dorothy."

"Forget it. I'll take my chances with a witch."

Before we got to Aunt Judith's condominium, she stopped at the Alderwood Mall, went into the Bon Marche, and came out with some big packages. I felt so low that I didn't even wonder what they were.

It wasn't until late in the afternoon, when she was helping me pack, that I found out what she had bought. It was a set of cinnamon-colored luggage with bright red zippers. "I like all-nylon," she said, "because it's light."

The luggage was very pretty, but I didn't tell her so. And I didn't thank her for the present.

After we'd zipped away the last of my things, Aunt Judith stood up. "We'd better get going. I told Margo we'd meet her at her house at six o'clock, and it will take us a good forty-five minutes to get there. I'll get my coat, and you check around to be sure we aren't leaving anything behind."

I checked around the canopy bed and gold chairs and in the carved desk. There wasn't a slipper or book left out. The room was as bare and picturelike as when I came.

On the way down the freeway to Everett and then over the trestle toward Lake Stevens, we didn't talk. I wanted to ask what the big mountain was ahead of us as we drove down Highway 92. I was wondering where Aunt Margo lived, but the hurt was burning inside me, and I wouldn't give in and ask. I just stared out the window as Aunt Judith drove along a woodsy road, turned off onto a long driveway, and pulled up in front of a small, brown, cedar-shaked house.

"I don't see any devil's-claw or skullcap there." Aunt Judith was looking at the flowers growing around the front porch.

"Very funny," I said coldly.

Aunt Margo's dark blue car came up beside us. It had a cardboard license in the back window. When we were out in front of the house, Aunt Judith asked if the car was brand-new.

"Yes," Aunt Margo answered. "I just got it last week."

I didn't exactly mean to say what I said next. It just came out of me. "I don't know what you need a new car for," I said. "Can't you just use your broom?"

"Copper Jones!" Aunt Judith drew back from me in horror.

Aunt Margo didn't even flinch.

Chapter
12

AFTER AUNT JUDITH HAD SPLIT IN A HURRY, AUNT
Margo helped me carry my bags into the house. "You'll
be sleeping in here," she said as we went toward the back
bedroom.

I dropped my load in the middle of the floor. "What
kind of a bed is that?" I hadn't meant to speak to her
again, but the bed on the floor surprised me so.

"That's a futon," she said.

"A what?"

"A Japanese futon. See. It has a thick cotton mattress
on wooden slats." She reached under the flowered quilt so
I could see the canvas-covered mattress lying on a raised
platform.

"It smells like an import store."

"I suppose so. It's the unbleached fabrics, I think." She
stared at me closely then. "It's your eyes. They're like
your father's. He was the best big brother to me. I remember when I was in college, and I didn't have much money
for clothes, he bought me a dress the color of spring green.
I loved that dress."

I gave her a cold stare back. She wasn't going to soften me up with stories about my dad.

"Well," she said, "you get unpacked, and I'll put some dinner on." She left the room before I could tell her I didn't want to eat.

By the time I had my clothes hung up in the closet, the smell of chicken pie reached my nose. I hadn't eaten breakfast and I hadn't eaten lunch with Aunt Judith. I decided, oh, well, and went into the big country kitchen. Not counting the bathroom, there were only four rooms in the house, a living room, two bedrooms, and the kitchen.

Hanging from the side of the kitchen cupboard was a string of garlic bulbs. I hoped we didn't get too much of that. The table was set with blue cotton place mats and white dishes. Blue flowers were in a copper pitcher in the center. The table itself was made of long boards with two wide strips of brass wrapped around them. I'd never seen anything like it.

With an oven-mitted hand, Aunt Margo put a ceramic bowl on my china plate. "I hope you're hungry." Chicken gravy bubbled around the piecrust covering the top of the bowl. I had really expected Swanson's chicken pie, like we would have gotten at Aunt Dorothy's.

Aunt Margo placed a bowl on her plate and a large dish of coleslaw between us. I tried the coleslaw first. It had pieces of tomato in it, but I was sure there was the faint taste of pickles, even though I didn't see any. "Pickles?" I mumbled.

"Dillweed," she said.

"What's devil's-claw and skullcap?"

"Herbs." She cut through the flaky piecrust with her fork, and the golden gravy oozed to the top. "Devil's-claw helps loosen your joints sometimes, and skullcap helps with visualizations."

I focused my eyes on the food before me. She must be a witch, I thought.

After dinner, I thought so even more when she asked me to take a walk with her to the river. We had to wind through the woods to get there. As we went along, I flipped my hands over some tall, leafy plants along the path.

"You'd better watch . . ." she started to say just before I let out a yowl.

I looked down at the palm of my hand where pink welts were rising. Aunt Margo didn't even check my stings. She stood in the middle of the path, turning her head this way and that, and muttered, "Next to the poison is the antidote.

"Ah, here it is." She reached up and broke a limb off a bush that had long, oval leaves. She bent a stem where the leaves branched out, took my hand in hers, and pressed the broken stem over a welt. She broke the stem several times more and smeared the juice on my palm until all the welts were covered.

"Remember this," she told me. "If you happen to touch a nettle, look for an elderberry bush. See, it has seven leaves coming off each stem."

I checked out the bush before I walked on down the path, keeping my hands carefully to my sides. When we were almost to the river, I stopped. "The pain's gone!" I looked at my palm. "The welts are gone!"

"Of course," she said. "And here we are. What do you think of the river?"

"It looks swift," I said.

"It is in some places. But see there where a log juts into the water? Right behind the log is a deep hole. That's where I go swimming every day it's warm."

It wasn't warm that day, because clouds kept drifting over the setting sun. I wondered if she would expect me to go swimming if it was warm the next evening. I didn't think I'd fit into her bathing suit. She wasn't big like Aunt Dorothy or potty like Brenda. But she wasn't trim like my mom and Aunt Judith, either. She was sort of round all over.

"Do you swim after dinner?" I asked her.

"No, I swim before dinner. Then I go up and pop something frozen in my microwave. I cook on the weekends for the whole week."

I'd wondered how she got that chicken pie done so fast. "Aunt Margo . . ." I hesitated. I didn't really want to be friendly with her, but curiosity kept getting the best of me. "What's that mountain up there behind the cliff?"

"Mt. Pilchuck. Named the same as the river." She turned to walk up the path through the woods. "And nobody calls me Margo, except people I don't know very well. Call me Maggie. Or Aunt Maggie, if you like."

Maggie? A witch named Maggie?

The phone rang as soon as we got in the house. It was my mother. By her voice, I could tell she was upset by my move, but she didn't give me any advice on how to get along this time. She said maybe I could come visit her next Sunday afternoon and that she missed me.

"I miss you, too," I told her.

I went on to bed after I hung up. I lay on the futon mattress and thought about her and Jeff and wondered what was going to happen to us. After a while, I switched to thinking about Aunt Judith, but that made me even more depressed. It hurt because she started out making me feel special and then got rid of me, fast. I turned on my side and tried to erase everybody out of my head.

I thought it would be a relief to drift off to sleep, but it wasn't. I had a horrible nightmare. I dreamed I was back under the bed at Aunt Judith's. Just as I started to sneeze, the burglar came into the room. He heard me and bent down and reached for me. I squirmed away. He grabbed me by one arm and yanked me out. I could see his black eyes burning in the dark. I struggled helplessly in his grip. He clutched my neck with one hand as his other hand slid over my chest, leaving me sickened with fear.

I awoke with my pajamas soaked in sweat.

In the morning, Aunt Maggie asked me how it felt to sleep on the futon. "The futon was OK," I told her. "But the nightmare I had wasn't."

She wanted to know every little detail about it. That was

strange. Nobody else had ever been interested in my night-mares. The breakfast was a little strange, too—boysenberry juice and homemade granola with toasted oats, almonds, and dates.

"The next time you have a nightmare, fight back," she said.

"You're kidding. He was twice as big as I am."

"It doesn't matter. Don't let anybody or anything hurt you in a dream. Scratch, bite, kick, make yourself have a knife and hack with all your strength." She buttered a piece of whole wheat toast. "The power you acquire in a dream seeps into your life."

"I'm sure," I said. "I'm twelve years old. I've been kicked out of three places. I'm sure I could 'acquire' the power to change that."

"You'd be surprised how much power you could have," she replied quietly.

I sat there trying to figure out just what she meant by that. Did she mean hexes? Or spells? But she interrupted my thoughts by saying we'd better be getting off to Lake Stevens Junior High.

We? "You're coming, too?" I asked.

"I want you to have an easy start," she said. "I know some people there."

She did, too. The secretary broke out in a big smile as soon as we came through the junior high office door. "Hi, Maggie," she said. "Who've you got there?"

"My niece, Copper Jones. She's staying with me. I want you to take good care of her."

"We will. We will. Hi, Copper."

I gave her a little smile back. New schools were making me nervous.

The secretary took the transfer papers I handed to her. While she was reading through the pages, another lady came through an inside door and stopped when she saw us. "Anath!" she cried out. "What are you doing here?"

"Registering my niece, Copper." My aunt went to the woman and they hugged.

"Ana . . . a . . . Maggie, we'll love having your niece. And we'll expect you to come to all the PTA meetings."

Aunt Maggie laughed. Me, I was trying to figure out this "Anath-Maggie" business. My aunt had two names?

The woman moved over to the counter and peered at my papers. "Seventh grade! Perfect. Put her in my homeroom," she told the secretary. "And give her Ruth Thompson for science. A new kid can use a kind heart."

After the secretary filled out my schedule, Aunt Maggie left, and I went with the teacher to her homeroom. Without even looking at my schedule, I figured out fast enough what her name was. "Hi, Ms. Treble. Hi, Ms. Treble," the kids all called out as we walked along the corridors.

More kids packed in against her when we got in the room. She had the class monitor find me a desk and mark it on the seating chart. Several kids smiled at me as I sat down. This was a switch!

So was class. It was supposed to be a social studies and language arts block. What Ms. Treble lectured about was time. "People regard time as being linear, in a line, in sequence. They think of one even minute after one even minute." She pointed to the chart above the blackboard that pictured the history of animals from dinosaurs to horses. "Is that the way time is, or is that just one view of time?"

Well, it's my view of time, I thought.

"Now, imagine that you are sitting at the bottom of a hill," she went on. "You are looking out at the road ahead of you. On that road is a red car. Is that red car in your past or present or future?"

"Present!" some of the kids called out.

"OK," she said. "Now, a yellow car had come by you a few seconds ago. That yellow car has gone around the curve of the hill and you can't see it anymore. Is the yellow car in your present time or past time?"

"Past," more kids yelled out.

"OK. Now, there is a black car around the curve to your left. You can't see it yet, but it is going to come in front of you in a few seconds. Is the black car—"

"Future!" we all answered before Ms. Treble could finish her question.

"You're sure?"

We all nodded.

"Now, just suppose that instead of sitting at the bottom of the hill, you were sitting on the top of the hill and could see the road curving to the right and left and you could see the black and red and yellow cars. Then all of the cars would be in your . . . ?"

"Present time." The boy in the seat beside me said.

"What if you were in an airplane?" a girl across the room asked.

"Then what?" Ms. Treble said.

"You're trying to say time isn't like a clock," the guy beside me blurted out. "That time and space are related."

"Well, what do you think?" she asked.

Beats me, I thought.

"Your class bell rings every fifty minutes," she said. "All your classes are an even amount of minutes. When you're in the classes, is that how you experience them?"

One girl raised her hand. That was a change. Ms. Treble nodded at her. "This class goes fast," the girl said. "And lunchtime does, but sixth-period math takes forever."

While the other kids told how fast or slow classes went for them, I was thinking about Aunt Dorothy's. On the days I was restricted to the bedroom, time crawled. When I was at the skating rink with Ricky, time flew. Whenever I was left alone at night, time crawled. I wondered how long the burglar had been in the condo. Under the bed, it had seemed like forever.

The teacher talked some more about our perception of time, and before I could even imagine fifty minutes being up, the bell rang, ending the period. The kids filtered out of the class slowly, arguing about whether or not a car's whole trip from Washington to Oregon would seem like the present if you were watching from the moon.

Mrs. Thompson's class was fourth period, just before lunch. While she called the roll, I wondered how long lunchtime would seem if I had to spend half of it in the girls' can.

I didn't have much time to worry, though, because this was a botany class and we were busy planting tulip bulbs in our individual pots. Most kids had brought their own pots from home, but Mrs. Thompson gave me one of hers to use. She was just like Ms. Treble said: kind to new kids.

Before the bell rang, and after our pots were neatly lined up on the counter, Mrs. Thompson asked where I lived. "On the Pilchuck River," I said. "East of Lake Stevens."

"Who lives near Copper?" she asked the class.

A girl with wild kinky hair the color of honey spoke up. "I do."

"Denise, will you take Copper to lunch?"

"Sure," Denise said.

Saved! No toilet stall for me in this school.

Chapter
13

DENISE AND I WALKED HOME FROM THE JUNIOR HIGH together. A cold wind was blowing against my denim jacket, and I wished it were lined with sheepskin. My right ear had begun to ache, so I pulled my collar up.

Denise kicked some leaves that had fallen along the road where we were walking. "I guess this is the end of summer. It was sure short enough."

"My aunt says she swims in the Pilchuck every warm night. I guess this is the end of that, too."

"Wait till you see the river in the winter," Denise said. "It comes way up to the banks, and if it rains for a long time, it floods the bottom of your aunt's land."

I hesitated before I crossed to the side of the road where Aunt Maggie lived. "You know my aunt?"

A sly smile flickered over Denise's face. "I know about her."

I nodded, told Denise I'd see her in the morning, and went on down the driveway to the house wondering what "know about her" meant.

When Aunt Maggie got home, I was on the futon bed with my right ear pressed against the pillow. She walked into my bedroom while she was still pulling her coat off. "You don't feel so good?"

"My ear aches."

She tossed the coat on the end of the bed and knelt down beside me. "Let me see."

She ran a hand slowly over my head and chest. She didn't touch me with the hand—just moved it around about an inch from my body. She seemed to be searching like a blind person would. Each time she passed over my ear, I felt a warmth.

She stood and flicked her hand several times as if shaking off something. "I think garlic in that ear would help."

Garlic?

I got out of the bed, put my shoes on, and followed her into the kitchen. She was at the counter cutting a clove of garlic in half. "Here," she said. "Put this gently into your ear."

"Won't I stink?" I asked.

"Would you rather have an earache?"

I pressed the half clove of garlic into my ear.

Dinner was homemade clam chowder and fruit salad. It was good, but I didn't feel like eating a whole lot. Halfway through my chowder, I put my spoon down and told Aunt Maggie I thought I'd go to bed.

It was after I went to the bathroom in the middle of the night that I had my next nightmare. I dreamed that I had been sent back to Aunt Dorothy's. She was mad about having me again and told me I'd have to sleep in the basement. The basement was gray, clammy, and dirty. The old blanket Aunt Dorothy had shoved into my hands, before she pushed me down the stairs, scratched the skin on my face.

When the morning light came through the dirty basement window, I heard Sarah call to me from the kitchen door. I got off the cot and walked barefoot across the cold floor and up the wooden stairs. Sarah poked a jar toward me. "Here's something to eat you," she said and went cackling into the kitchen, locking the door behind her.

I thought she had said, "Here's something for you to eat," so I opened the jar as I went back down the steps. A huge, hairy spider jumped out. I screamed in terror, the jar crashed onto the cement, and the spider leaped for me. I frantically brushed and brushed at my pajamas, trying to keep the spider away.

Just as the spider crawled onto my face, I woke up.

For the rest of the night, I stayed awake, thinking of Aunt Dorothy and Sarah and hating them. I hated how they looked, and I hated how they acted. And I hated how they treated me. If I were a witch, I could get all kinds of slimy, rotting, ripping, bloody revenges on them.

By the time breakfast was ready, I had my plan. I sat down at the table as innocently as possible. When Aunt Maggie asked how my ear felt, I said it was better. I didn't say I had taken the garlic out before I had my shower. I didn't say I didn't want to stink at school.

What I said was "Are you a witch?"

Aunt Maggie looked at me calmly as she drank her carrot juice. "Yes, I am."

"Then you know how to do hexes, right? Stick pins in a doll?"

This time she put her glass down and paused longer before she answered. "Yes, I suppose I do. And I think you mean a poppet."

"OK, stick pins in a poppet." I leaned across the table. "Will you teach me how?"

"Do you mean teach you how to cast a curse on someone?"

I nodded. "Yep."

"No, I won't," she said.

I sat straight up in my chair. "Why not?"

"Because I believe that what you put out is what you get back—three times stronger."

"Why?"

"Because it's your energy, and it returns to you. Just like a boomerang. Hexing someone you don't like will harm you more than it harms them."

"So," I said. "If a person was out to hurt you, you would just let them?"

"No, if I believed someone was really intent on hurting me, I would bind them."

"What does that do?"

"Prevents them from doing harm. And then what came back would protect me from doing harm."

Big deal. I finished up my hot oatmeal and went off to school. I didn't think Maggie was much of a witch.

School was all right. I had Denise to eat lunch with. But by the afternoon, my ear was hurting again. I decided not to wait while Denise picked up her sick brother's homework.

I was already going out the school's front door when I stopped still, causing two pissed-off kids to bump into me. I had remembered my tulips, and that it was Friday.

I pushed back through the crowd and made my way to Mrs. Thompson's room. She was still there, cleaning potting soil off the counter. "I thought I'd better water my pot," I told her, "so the bulbs don't dry out over the weekend."

"Good girl." She gave my head a pat after she dumped the dirty paper towels into the wastebasket beside the sink. "You have the prettiest hair, Copper. My mother's was the same color."

I concentrated on circling the tap water around the inside edge of my pot. "I guess that's enough." I was chattering away to make up for my self-consciousness. "Just so the energy I put into these bulbs comes back in beautiful flowers."

"What have you been doing, watching *Star Wars*?" It was a boy's voice behind me.

I turned around, still holding my dripping pot. A boy and girl were sitting in chairs beside Mrs. Thompson's desk. Or the girl was sitting. The boy had his chair tipped back with his feet on the seat in front of him. I hadn't seen them when I came in.

Mrs. Thompson sat down at her desk, too. "Copper,

this is Faith and this is Jake. They were my students last year. They're down to visit me from the high school."

"Oh, hi." I wiped the bottom of my pot and put it on its saucer on the counter. I was going to hurry out of the room so I didn't interrupt their visit.

But Mrs. Thompson said, "Sit down and join us."

"Ya," Jake said, watching me with his black eyes until I eased into the nearest chair. "What's this about putting energy into your bulbs?"

"Well," I said, "I live with a witch. She's my aunt, and she claims everything you do acts like a boomerang."

The girl Faith raised her eyebrows. "A witch? That's interesting."

"You mean," Jake said, " 'What goes around comes around'?"

"Or," Mrs. Thompson added, " 'As ye sow, so shall ye reap.' "

Faith turned her attention to Mrs. Thompson. "You go to that white church with the steeple and the bell, don't you? I saw you out front one Sunday when we were driving through Machias."

Mrs. Thompson nodded. "Yes, did you know the Machias Historical Society had that old church restored this year. A young contractor who lives on the Pilchuck River made it as good as new."

"I live on the Pilchuck River," I said. "Or my aunt does."

"What kind of a witch is she?" Faith wanted to know. "A black witch or a white witch?"

"Beats me. Are there different colors?" I asked Mrs. Thompson.

"Beats me, too," she said. "I've never met a witch."

"Well, what does she do?" Faith persisted.

"Not much," I said. "I don't think she's much of a witch. She doesn't believe in hexing, and all she'll do to bad people is bind them, whatever that is, and all she's done to me is take nettle stings away with elderberry stems and put garlic in my aching ear."

"In the war, Russians put garlic in the soldiers' wounds so their wounds wouldn't get infected," Mrs. Thompson told us. "Garlic contains a natural antibiotic."

"It does?" I said.

"She's a white witch," Faith stated firmly, like she knew what she was talking about.

I looked from one person to the next, bewildered. "How do you tell a white witch from a black witch?"

"Same as you tell good people from bad people, I guess," Jake said. "By what they do. If they're into evil practices and want you to do things you know you shouldn't do, they ain't good!"

Faith nodded her head slowly. "I know some good people with little powers, and they're just like your aunt, very careful about what they send out."

"I'm not sure if my aunt has any powers."

"How long have you lived with her?"

"Just a couple days."

Faith and Jake both laughed. I had the feeling they knew things I didn't know. Not that their laugh was mean.

Just that they both were in on something that I wasn't.

"Listen," Faith said, "if your aunt's a real witch, she'll have her powers all right."

"Well, I guess I'll find out." I got up to leave. My ear was really hurting. "I'll see you Monday, Mrs. Thompson. I hope I see you guys again, too."

"So do I," Faith said. "I'd like to meet your aunt."

Chapter
14

AUNT MAGGIE OPENED THE DOOR OF MY BEDROOM slowly that Saturday morning. "You're awake," she said when she saw me watching her from my pillow.

"I wish I weren't," I said back.

She came over and sat on the edge of my bed. "Ear still hurts?"

I nodded.

"How'd you sleep?"

"Mostly I didn't, and when I did, I had more of those gross nightmares."

"What happened this time?"

"Well." I turned over on my back. "The burglar was in the room and I got a gun."

"Good," Aunt Maggie said.

"Sure. And when I shot the gun at him, the bullet went out about two feet and then drooped down to the ground."

"And then what did you do?"

"I ran. What do you think?"

"No, never run, Copper. Kick, scratch, bite, but fight

until you beat the nightmare back. And when you wake up, if you haven't completely won, make up an ending to the dream with you coming out victorious."

"Sure." I started to turn back onto my side, but Aunt Maggie reached out and held me by my shoulder.

"Let me see if there is something I can do for that ear." She sat very still a minute, seeming to look out into space, and then slowly moved her hand around the side of my head. She never touched my ear, but I could feel warmth coming from her hand.

When she stopped, she sat still again. "Copper," she finally said, "what would make you feel safe at night?"

"Easy," I answered her. "A real gun that works."

"I can't get you a gun," she said, like she really thought I meant it. "You're too young for a license. What else would make you feel secure?"

It was my turn to be quiet a minute. "A phone. Right here beside me. Then if I'm alone at night and I hear someone, I can call the cops right away."

"I'm not going to leave you alone, Copper, but a phone's easy anyway. I'll order a jack on Monday and have it installed on the wall by your bed." She stood up. "No problem. Now rest, and I'll bring you some breakfast."

"I'm not that sick," I told her.

"The more you rest, the faster your ear infection will clear up."

So I rested all day and ate in bed and listened to the sounds of Aunt Maggie cooking her weekly dinners in the kitchen. I slept sometimes, and I slept all night, and in the morning my earache was gone.

Aunt Maggie didn't seem surprised, but I was. After breakfast, I jumped up from the table and said I'd do the dishes. I wanted to be useful. And I didn't want to get kicked out again, either.

While I cleaned the kitchen, Aunt Maggie spread some strange-looking cards out on the table. They had weird pictures on them, like a man hanging upside down with a yellow halo around his head, and a woman petting a lion, and a man in a hooded cloak holding up a lighted lantern. She had the cards laid out in a cross with a row beside it and sat staring at them.

When I couldn't stand it anymore, I stopped sweeping around the table and leaned on my broom. "What are you doing?"

She looked up at me as if she'd forgotten anyone was in the room. "Seeing how we'll turn out."

Uh-oh. "And what are you finding?" I asked cautiously.

"That maybe it will be a little while before you will trust me and I can trust you."

I didn't know exactly what she meant, but I decided I might be better off sweeping than asking questions.

After she had put the cards away and I had taken out the garbage, she suggested that we drive out to see my mother. That idea made me even more nervous than I was already. I knew my mom thought Aunt Maggie was evil. Maybe the cards couldn't trust me, but I sure couldn't trust my mother's moods.

Aunt Maggie chatted cheerfully about the red and orange leaves on the vine maples as she drove along the roads. I hardly listened to her. The nearer we got to the alcoholic treatment center, the more I squirmed in my seat.

Aunt Maggie must have noticed. "You know, Copper," she said, "if your mother acts nice today, it will be because she wants to."

"I know."

"And," she went on, "if your mother doesn't act nice today, it will be her choice."

I kept my face turned toward the passenger's window and didn't answer that one. She didn't know my mother very well. Sometimes I could get my mom laughing and she would forget she was mad, or I could bring up something interesting real quick and she would forget to feel sad.

Sad, mad, mad, sad, I said silently to the window. I hoped my mom wouldn't get sad or mad that day. I promised myself I wouldn't say anything to set her off.

I did, though.

The receptionist had us wait in the lobby while she called my mom's room. It was quite a few minutes before Mom came in to greet us. She looked sleepy. "I wasn't expecting you so soon," she said after she hugged me.

"I guess we are a few hours early." I sat back down on the couch with Aunt Maggie and patted the empty cushion beside me.

Aunt Maggie spoke up. "It was my suggestion that we come right after breakfast."

"Oh." My mother looked my aunt over silently, then

tossed her head to the side in that way she has of letting you know she's decided to put up with something she doesn't like. "All right, then, let's go back to my room."

"No, no. We can talk here." I patted the cushion again and glanced up at Mom expectantly. To my relief, she joined us.

I waited. And waited. Searched my mind frantically for a safe subject, but none came. Mom concentrated on jangling her bracelets up and down her arm. Aunt Maggie sat quietly, looking calm and pleasant like she always does.

"Well, well," I jumped in, "suppose you were at the bottom of a hill and a yellow car had just gone by on the road in front of you. Would that car be in your future, present, or past?"

"Past, I guess." Mom looked at me questioningly, as if she expected this to be a riddle.

"And then there was a red car coming from around the curve of the hill, but you couldn't see it. Would that car be in your present, past, or future?"

Aunt Maggie had turned to me with a knowing smile, but she didn't say anything.

Mom shrugged. "Past, I suppose." She wasn't too interested, but I had her attention, so I went through the whole "the future is now" bit. And when I finished that, I told her about Denise, the river, and everything else I could think of, except witches.

When I wound down, Mom turned to my aunt. "Of course, Jeff will pay for Copper's room and board, but I want to thank you for taking her. It seems my own sisters were too busy with their lives to bother with her."

"She's good company for me," Aunt Maggie said.

Mom patted my arm. "She is that."

I relaxed against the back of the couch while Mom asked Aunt Maggie about her work and Aunt Maggie told about being a manager of a computer section.

"I wouldn't even try to work one of those machines," Mom said.

"It must be about time for your lunch." I reached over to hug her good-bye, wanting to get out of there while she was still in a good mood. "Even if we came early, I got to see you."

She gave her tinkly laugh and hugged me back. "Well, Copper-baby, I don't look my best when I just wake up."

"Oh, you always look pretty," I told her as Aunt Maggie and I stood up. "You'll be finished with your treatment in about two weeks?"

"Maybe a bit longer than that. But"—she looked up at me with a bright expression—"when I do get out of here, we'll go down to Jeff and have a wonderful party. I'll be drinking sparkling cider, of course."

My mind flashed on Jeff's saying he didn't want to party with my mom anymore, and I blurted out, "Mom, maybe Jeff . . . Maybe it would be better if we didn't plan on a party. Maybe you could think about working." As the lines in her face hardened, I panicked and laughed wildly. "Only not on computers, of course."

"What are you talking about? What do you want me to do? Get a job at Penney's?"

I waved my hands in front of me to fend off her anger. "No, no, I meant . . . Maybe it would be better to just make a nice dinner for Jeff instead of a party."

"And would you like me to wear a Mother Hubbard apron, too?" Her voice was getting louder.

The receptionist got up from her desk and came over to us. "Cassandra, is this your daughter? I think I saw her when she came in a few weeks ago."

Mom pulled herself together enough to introduce us all around. I got out of there then and beat Aunt Maggie to the car. I crouched in the passenger's seat while she climbed in. "I was only trying to warn her. Jeff told me he couldn't work and party with Mom, too."

Aunt Maggie turned on the ignition, backed the car out of the parking place, and headed down the wooded driveway. "You aren't responsible for your mother, Copper."

"I know, but I didn't want to make her mad."

"Maybe she's frightened of the future."

That was a big help. If my mom was scared, what would happen to me? I spent the rest of the ride home staring out the window and rubbing my aching neck.

By the time Aunt Maggie and I sat down to lunch, my neck was really hurting. She noticed, of course. Probably because I kept wiggling my head around trying to stretch the pain away.

"It always seems to get stiff after Mom's upset," I explained.

"Perhaps you could still love your mother without getting entangled in her problems," she suggested.

"Some people say that I'm just like her," I said.

Aunt Maggie nodded. "I think most kids tend to imitate their parents. The tricky part is to decide which things you want to copy and which things will only make your life harder if you imitate them."

"Who's supposed to be my model, then?" I snapped back. "A witch?" A witch. A witch. A witch. The words repeated in my ears. I sounded just like my mother.

I glanced at my aunt fearfully, but she didn't seem to be mad. She only said quietly that I could look around for somebody who seemed to have a life I admired. I thought of Mrs. Thompson.

Before I went to bed that night, Aunt Maggie told me to take a shower and let the hot water beat down on my neck. "That might loosen up those tense muscles."

It didn't. Or at least it didn't enough for me to go to sleep. I turned on my side, then my back, then my other side. After about an hour, I got up to ask for an aspirin.

Instead of giving me one, my aunt said, "Sit over there in that straight chair."

I sat down in the chair facing her writing desk. She came to stand behind me. I didn't look back, but I could feel her standing there. Then I felt her hands on my shoulders. Her hands squeezed gently at first, then harder and harder. Then very gradually her hands loosened their grip, and as they did, a great whoosh swept off my neck and shoulders.

"Oh. Oh. Oh!" I said. I felt like a balloon that someone had suddenly untied, letting all the air rush out.

I wiggled my head this way and that. It moved easily. The stiffness was gone. The pain was gone. I turned in my seat. "How did you do that? How did you do that? What did you do?"

She smiled her sweet, calm smile and said, "Oh, we just released some of the energy that was caught in there."

Chapter
15

I SLEPT SO SOUNDLY SUNDAY NIGHT THAT AUNT MAG-gie had to shake me to wake me up. I lay there awhile, looking out at the lacy branches of the cedar tree framed by the gray-white sky. The second time Aunt Maggie came in my room she was scowling with impatience.

"Hurry up or we're going to be late." She waited until I had thrown my covers off before she turned quickly to leave.

"Hey, wait a minute," I said. I wanted to ask her a million questions about how she got rid of the pain in my neck.

She turned back briefly. "I haven't time to wait. I've got a job to get to. Now, get up fast."

I did. What was making her so crabby? "You're sure crabby this morning," I told her between gulps of my orange juice.

She was putting on her coat and handing me my lunch money at the same time. "If I agree to be somewhere at a certain hour, I want to be there."

My face must have wilted at her sharp tone, because she shook my chin gently after she pulled me out the door with her. "I'll see you tonight," she said and dashed for her car.

Denise was leaning against the fence in front of her house. "You're late enough," she told me.

"I was poky getting up, and it made my aunt mad," I said. "But wait till I tell you what she did to me last night." I told Denise everything, even about my dumb remark to my mom. Denise and I were getting to be friends.

"You know," she said as we hurried up the hill to the school, "your aunt's a witch."

"I know," I told her, "but how did you know?"

"Well"—she took my hand and pulled me closer so the passing kids couldn't hear her—"one evening this summer, I was walking through the woods with my dog, and I saw your aunt. She was carrying a swordlike knife and a big, black iron pot. I thought, wow, this is weird, and followed her.

"We didn't go very far before she met another woman. Your aunt called the woman Isis, and the woman called your aunt Anat or something."

"They must choose weird names for themselves," I said. "Anyway, my aunt's is Anath."

"Ya, that's what it sounded like."

We were on the playfield by then, and some other girls joined us, so Denise whispered to me, "Tell you the rest after school."

I went on into Ms. Treble's class. She gave us the assignment of writing a description of what we imagined our life would be like if the ozone layer above the north pole disappeared. I tried to write a sensible essay about ice melting and oceans rising, but I kept thinking about my first day in the office. Ms. Treble had called my aunt Anath. So Ms. Treble must be a witch, too. And Mrs. Thompson thought she'd never met one!

I was still thinking about this when I got to Mrs. Thompson's botany class. But not for long. She had a way of sucking you right into the world of flowers and trees. Only this hour it was fungi. Some fungi are parasites, or parasitic, as she called it. Like ringworm and rust and athlete's foot. And some are beneficial like those that produce antibiotics. But what we were going to study was mushrooms. We were going to learn to identify the poisonous ones and the nonpoisonous ones.

"How about those little, wet, brown ones that make you happy?" the boy sitting beside me asked with a grin.

Mrs. Thompson looked over her glasses at him and shook her head. "I think we'll skip by those, Wayne."

All the kids laughed.

"What we do need," she went on, "is a wet meadow and woods where we can collect our specimens."

Denise raised her hand. "Copper's aunt has a big woods below her house."

"Do you think your aunt would let us go on a field trip there?" Mrs. Thompson asked me.

"I think she would," I said.

"You ask her tonight, and if it's all right with her, bring me a note tomorrow. Tell her we'd like to come on Friday."

"OK," I agreed.

"That will be a blast getting out of school and going to your place on Friday," Denise said on our walk home. "And I'll be able to show you just where the witches had their ceremony."

"Was it dark out?" I asked.

"Not at first, but when it got dark, there was a full moon and I could see most everything. But I couldn't hear everything because I was on the hill above the river and they were down below in a clearing."

We were almost to Denise's house by then. I slowed down and looked her in the face. "Tell me exactly what you saw."

"Well, I think your aunt's the leader. There was a fire in the pot, and the witches were around it in a big circle. They were holding hands. I didn't see how the pot was lit because I was trying to hold Susie, my dog, down so she wouldn't make any noise.

"Then your aunt takes her big knife and goes to one side and calls something out and traces the shape of a star in the air. Then she does that on all four sides. And then she puts the tip of her sword in the fire in the pot and another witch takes a candle and lights it from the fire and carries the candle around the outside of the circle and lights the other candles which are poked into the ground."

"Whoa." I'd stopped still in the road. "And then what happened?"

Denise shrugged. "Susie got loose and ran down the bank, and I got scared and split."

"Ohh!" I slouched against her fence in disappointment.

"But don't worry. All you have to do is watch your aunt, and any evening you see her with a big, black pot, call me, and we'll follow them again. I think the moon's getting bigger. I think they do it on a full moon, so it should be pretty soon."

"Have you told anybody else about this?"

"Just my mom," Denise said. "She said I wasn't supposed to go blabbing about it. She said people hear the word 'witch' and remember all the terrible things they've read about cults. She said most people don't know there are good witches."

"I told Mrs. Thompson about Aunt Maggie," I said.

"Well, you better not tell anybody else."

"I think maybe Ms. Treble is one, too."

"Don't tell on her, either." Denise picked a dandelion and blew its seeds into the air before she continued. "It's dumb, though. Ms. Treble is so nice. My mom says she likes to live next to a good witch because you can depend on them. They always tell the truth."

"Why is that?"

"Mom explained it to me, but I didn't get it all. It has something to do with making spells work. After your aunt moved in, my mom got a book on witches, but it was too complicated for me."

I wished I had a book on witches. After I left Denise, I thought about what she had said all the way home. I wasn't surprised that Aunt Maggie didn't lie. But my mom sure lied. Especially about how much she'd been drinking.

When I got in the house, I plunked down my Pee Chee and took off my jacket, and I was going to plunk myself down on the futon when I saw the phone. The phone was sitting right on the brass chest beside the bed. I sat on the bed to look it over closely.

I was a little disappointed that it wasn't a pay phone or a cat phone like my cousins and I had seen in Spencer's. The only thing unusual about this one was the red-orange numbers on the buttons. Wait a minute! I unplugged it from the jack and took it in the closet. The numbers glowed in the dark. Aw right!

While I was deciding who to call first, I went in the kitchen to get something to eat. I cut a couple slices off Aunt Maggie's homemade whole wheat bread and smeared them with butter and her thick jam that had lumps of peaches and apricots and curled slivers of lemon in it. After I carried the bread into the bedroom and set it on the chest, I licked my sticky fingers before I poked out Johanna's number.

This was the first time since I'd left Seattle that I felt like calling one of my old friends. Part of me couldn't wait to tell Johanna that I lived with a witch and part of me kept remembering what Denise had said about keeping my mouth shut. I never got to say anything, though. The phone rang and rang and nobody answered.

I poked out Brenda's number. Sarah answered. Her voice sounded like a little girl's, not like the cackling thing that had given me a spider in the basement. She said,

"Wait just a minute. Brenda's making herself a sandwich."

While I waited, I imagined Brenda's sandwich. It would be made of cottony white bread with thin store jelly.

"Hi," Brenda said.

"Hi," I said. "My Aunt Maggie just bought me a phone for my bedroom, so I thought I'd give you a call."

"Wow, cool. What's it like?"

I told her about the numbers that shone in the dark, and then we talked about school, and then before we said good-bye I surprised myself by thanking her for being nice to me when I was at her house. I guess this surprised her, too, and she mumbled something about wishing the whole visit had been nice.

After I hung up, I lay back on the futon, eating and thinking of my cousins. Brenda was like her father, decent. Sarah was going to turn out just like Aunt Dorothy and everybody would hate her and she would never know why. And Kim. Kim hadn't seemed to copy either of her folks until she got in trouble, and then she blamed me just like her mother did.

It was awful when I was there, but it was OK here, and I wasn't going to blow it. I swallowed the last bite of bread, licked my fingers again, bounced off the bed, and went into the kitchen to do the breakfast dishes and set the table. I straightened up Aunt Maggie's messy cupboards, too.

Aunt Maggie got home late. She had taken her lunch hour, and then some, to come home when the phone was installed. I wanted to hug her for giving it to me, but I was too shy. Instead I told her how neat it was about ten times. While we were eating dinner, I asked her what those cards were that she'd had on the table Saturday.

"Tarot cards," she said.

"Will you teach me to play them?"

She laughed. "I don't think you could say you play them."

I pulled the cheesy strings of lasagna up with my fork until they broke apart. "What, then?"

"They help you concentrate on a question."

"Like fortune-telling."

She laughed again. "No. More like a guide to another way of knowing the world around you."

I put down my fork. "Well, will you teach me?"

"Someday perhaps." She wasn't laughing now. "I think you need to understand yourself better before you try to acquire powers. Otherwise, it may do you more harm than good."

"Well, how could . . ." I searched around in my head for an example. "How could knowing how to take someone's headache away hurt me?"

"Easy. Unless you know how to protect yourself, you'll get the headache."

This was making me mad. Whenever you really want to learn something, adults always make it some mysterious secret that you can't have. "So I don't get to know until I'm bigger," I said nastily and went about eating my dinner.

"That's not correct," she answered me quietly. "First

you learn how to face your fears and be strong enough to tell the truth."

I looked at her over the the rim of my glass of milk. "And just how do I start that?"

"You can start by getting a hold on your nightmares." She got up from the table to get our dessert.

"I probably won't have anymore with the phone beside me," I said to her back.

She put our bowls of blackberry cobbler on the table and took her seat. "Perhaps. But you should be able to control your regular dreams, too."

Control my dreams? "Sure," I said.

She poured cream over her cobbler—something my slim mother would never have done. "They're your dreams."

"I know, but they're dreams."

"Fine. Tell yourself that before you go to sleep, and if anything happens in them you don't like, change it."

"You're kidding."

"No I'm not. How do you expect to shape other things in the world until you can shape your own dreams?"

She had me there. So when I went to bed that night, I told myself that because they were mine, I could change my dreams if I wanted to. And guess what happened? Nothing.

"It didn't work," I told Aunt Maggie at breakfast. "In fact, I could only remember little bits of my last dream when I woke up. Something about Mrs. Thompson and mushrooms."

"Good. You tried and you remembered part of a dream. Try again tonight. Say to yourself that you will be aware you're dreaming, when you dream."

I ate my oatmeal. No use arguing with her. To tell the truth, I was beginning to think she was more than a little strange.

"Oh!" I had suddenly remembered the field trip. "Could Mrs. Thompson bring our botany class down here Friday afternoon to identify mushrooms?"

"Yes," my aunt said.

"Then you're supposed to write her a note that it's OK."

"All right, I will. And there's another thing. I have to go to a retirement dinner for one of my workers Friday night."

"That's fine. I can stay here with my phone." I got up to put my bowl and glass in the sink.

She got up to get a pen and paper. When I was ready to leave for school, she handed me the note. "I don't want you to stay alone. I want you to go with me, but I know it will be boring, so think of something you'd like to do afterward. I'll trade you for doing something with me for my doing something with you. A show. Or a new sweater. Or anything you'd like."

I thought of her little proposition on the way over to Denise's. I knew what I wanted to do Friday night. I wanted to go alone to the skating rink in Marysville to see Ricky Layton. But how could I maneuver that?

Chapter
16

ON THURSDAY NIGHT, JUST BEFORE I WENT TO BED, Aunt Maggie brought up the retirement dinner again. She was sitting on my futon, and I was pulling on my pajamas. "Have you decided what you'd like to do after the dinner tomorrow night?" she asked me.

I turned my back to her while I hung up my clothes. "Why don't you just drop me off in Marysville before the dinner, and I'll go to a show with one of my friends?"

"I'd rather have you with me," she said.

"Yes, but it doesn't make sense." I was taking my time folding my jeans over a hanger. "You said the dinner would be boring for me and it would be boring for you to see a teenage movie, so just drop me off and pick me up in the same place and we can go home together. Simple. Right?"

"Copper, turn around."

I turned around.

"Now tell me what you really want to do."

"I'd like to see my friends in Marysville, and we can go to a movie, and if you're so worried about it, you can pick out the movie—"

"Copper, something is wrong. You're talking fast and your voice is way up high." She was looking into my eyes.

"Well, I'm fixing it so we both can have a good time. Aw right, Auntie?" I stopped in the middle of a tinkly laugh. The laugh was my mother's.

There was silence. I wiggled uncomfortably under Aunt Maggie's steady gaze. She was sitting on my bed, so I couldn't get in it. There was nothing else for me to do but stand in front of her.

After I stood there for what seemed an hour, I blurted out, "You wouldn't let me do what I want, anyway."

"How do you know?" she asked. "Is it something that will hurt you?"

"No, it won't hurt me at all. You'll just think it will."

"Try me."

So I told her. I told her about wanting to go to the skating rink and skate with Ricky Layton and that he was a nice boy in my grade, and I told her, too, that there'd be some stoners there, but they just hung around in their black Mötley Crüe T-shirts and didn't bother anybody.

When I finished, she said, "I'll tell you what. You take a book along to my dinner, and after you eat, you can go out in the lobby and read so you don't have to listen to the speeches. I'll take a book to the skating rink and sit off to the side where no one will notice me."

"You're serious?" I asked.

"I'm serious," she said.

On Friday afternoon, Mrs. Thompson had each of us students take a trowel for digging, wax paper to wrap around the mushrooms, and a box to carry them in. We trooped through the mushy, wet ground of Aunt Maggie's lower field and on to the woods. When we were halfway to the river, Mrs. Thompson said, "I'll stop here and sit on this stump. You all spread out and see what you can find. Everybody come back in about fifteen minutes."

Denise and I went off together. We went through the trees, down a bank, and onto flat meadow that bordered the river. "This is where the witches met," Denise said.

"Hmmm." I looked around. It was a pretty place all right. And private. A wooded bank on one side and a cliff across the river.

"And," Denise went on, "I looked on our calendar and there's a full moon tomorrow night. They're sure to have another meeting."

"I don't know. She hasn't said anything about being gone tomorrow night, and she makes a big thing about my not being left alone."

"Well, if she does say she has a meeting or something, tell her you'll stay all night with me."

"She doesn't buy lies," I said.

"It won't be a lie. I'll tell my mom I've asked you over. It will be fun anyway."

I agreed it would be fun, but I had that uneasy feeling

I was about to do the wrong thing again. "Let's look for some mushrooms," I said quickly, to make the feeling go away.

We found a group of yellow ones climbing up a dead tree. I looked in Aunt Maggie's book I was carrying. "They're Clustered Woodlovers, I think. It says here that they taste bitter."

"Let's take samples for our collection just the same."

Next we found some old puffballs that were caving in. Then, while Denise gathered up some skinny, tan mushrooms, I came upon some big, cream-colored ones with brown scales. I remembered reading something about those in the book. I sat on the wet grass and looked through the pictures. I was right! The Prince!

"I found The Prince!" I yelled at Denise.

She came over to stand beside me, twisting her samples into the wax paper. "You can't be sure until you let the spores drop on white paper. And anyway, you're not supposed to dig up so many."

"I'm just picking the three big ones," I told her, stuffing them in my box. "Let's get back and show them to Mrs. Thompson." I flew up the bank and through the woods and dropped at Mrs. Thompson's feet, holding my box out to her. "Look. The Prince."

"Copper, you're right. What a lucky find. They're delicious. Your aunt will love them." She tried to pass my box back to me.

I pushed it into her lap. "No, you take them. We're going out to dinner tonight."

She tilted her head at me. "You could eat them tomorrow night."

"No, there's some more little ones coming up for us."

"Well," she said, "you talked me into it. They're one of my favorites."

I felt all warm inside that I could do something for her. I wasn't so warm outside, though, so I moved off the damp ground onto the fallen log Denise was sitting on. "I've been wondering," I said to Mrs. Thompson, "about that Faith and Jake who visited you."

"Oh, Faith," she said. "She's an interesting girl. She can meditate and see what people are doing. We used to call those people clairvoyants. I guess they call the process remote viewing now. Faith and Jake believed a teacher was stealing last year, and Faith followed him in her mind's eye."

"I remember that," Denise put in. "It was in the papers and everything."

"No wonder she wanted to meet my aunt," I said.

The other kids started coming back with their mushrooms then. I was a little disappointed. I liked having Mrs. Thompson's attention. But she showed everyone my Prince mushrooms, and that was kinda neat. Wayne said, "Wow, they must be six inches across."

On the way to the retirement dinner in Everett, we had to drive through the little town of Machias. I pointed out Mrs. Thompson's church to Aunt Maggie. "Oh, yes," she said. "I was glad they saved that building. There aren't many little white churches with belfries and spires anymore." After she drove on a minute, she asked, "Would you like to go to that church some Sunday?"

"I was just talking about it because Mrs. Thompson goes there," I explained.

"You could go, too, if you wanted. It's too far to walk, but I'd be glad to take you."

I thought that over. Her taking me? "Can you go to church?"

She glanced over at me, giving me a very small smile. "I don't think they throw witches out."

I tried to smile, too, but it didn't seem funny. What seemed weird was her talking right out about being a witch. I just couldn't get used to it.

The dinner was in a private dining room in the Everett Pacific Hotel. It was as boring as Aunt Maggie said it would be. I was glad when I could escape to the hotel lobby and read my book, *The Murder of Hound Dog Bates.* It was about a boy who lived with three aunts, and when his dog got killed, he tried to figure out which aunt did it. If I had a dog, I know which of my aunts would murder it.

I was so involved in the story, I jumped when Aunt Maggie came up to me and said she was ready to go. I reluctantly closed my book, hating to leave Sassafras Bates's world—until I remembered Ricky Layton.

He wasn't there when we arrived at the skating rink. At least, I couldn't see him in the crowd. It made a little worry knot of disappointment in my stomach.

Aunt Maggie chose a table behind the refreshment bar

and sat in a chair that had its back to the skaters. That was tactful of her. In fact, she was a nice person. Really nice, I thought, not phony-nice like my Aunt Judith.

I skated slowly around the rink, feeling a little sick with the disappointment. All my lying to Aunt Maggie was for nothing?

Strong, hard hands grabbed my waist from behind, and I was zipped across the floor to the far corner and whirled around to look at Ricky Layton's huge grin. He took his hands from my waist and put them against the wall, one on each side of my head. "I thought you wouldn't show up again," he said. "Kim told my brother you got kicked out of her house for coming here."

"I did, but I'm living with another aunt now, and she brought me."

"Aw right!" His face was about three inches from mine, and his nearness made me shy. I tried to glance sideways at the other skaters, but he said, "Hey, let me see those wolf's eyes."

When I turned my head back to him, he asked, "Did you miss me?"

"Uh huh."

"Well, show me."

I just didn't know what to do while he was looking at me so intently. I tried to glance away again. He took my chin in his hand, bent closer, and kissed me. Hard. On the lips.

When he drew back, he smiled and said, "Hello, Copper."

"Hello, Ricky," I whispered.

We skated then, holding hands. Circling around and around the rink. Me following him in a dizzy daze.

Too soon, his brother tapped Ricky on the shoulder and told him it was time to split. The three of us sat together taking off our skates. When they got up to go, Ricky said, "See you again?"

I nodded.

"Promise?"

I nodded.

He touched my cheek quickly before he went off with his brother.

I didn't say much to Aunt Maggie while we were walking out to her car. But when she was driving back through Everett, she asked, "Well, did you have a good time?"

"He kissed me."

"How was it?"

"Oh, OK." You can't tell your aunt everything.

"Your first kiss?"

"First time with a boy." That sounded funny. Like I'd kissed girls. "I mean other than my mother." That started me thinking of my mom. "What do you suppose will happen to my mom?"

"I don't know," she said thoughtfully. "I don't know when she'll decide to take the responsibility for her life."

"Kids can't depend on just themselves."

"She's not a kid. And anyway, kids can be responsible for their own actions."

I didn't particularly want to talk about that, so I asked her, "Why don't witches lie?"

"Because witches expect something to happen when they say it will. Lies would rob their words of power." She paused as she slowed the car for a red light, and then went on, "Suppose that I told you I'd take you to a movie on Saturday, but when Saturday came, I said I'm sorry, but I've made other plans. Then what would my word mean?"

Aunt Maggie shifted into gear and drove on down to Highway 92. "Suppose I also lie and say the film we were going to see is no longer at the movie theater, anyway. Later, suppose I visit someone who has the flu, and I tell myself I will remain healthy. But how can I believe I won't get the flu just because I say I won't, when I'm a liar and I know I'm a liar?"

"You mean if I don't tell the truth, I can't cast a spell."

"Correct," she said.

Forget that, then, I thought to myself. "What about this remote viewing? Can witches see people who aren't around?"

She was turning into our driveway and paid attention to parking the car before she answered me. "Sometimes. When they're in a trance. When they look into a crystal, we call it scrying."

"And I suppose you wouldn't teach me to do that?"

"Copper, before you learn to play a song on a guitar, you learn the chords first. How's your dreaming going?"

"Nowhere," I said.

So that night, I tried to tell myself to remember to remember when I was dreaming, but my mind slipped away to imagining the next time I was with Ricky Layton.

Chapter
17

IN THE MORNING, WHILE I WAS HELPING AUNT MAGGIE cut up a boiled chicken, the phone rang. Aunt Maggie answered it. "It's for you," she said when she came back in the kitchen.

"I'll take it in my room." Whoa, this is cool, I thought, as I closed my bedroom door.

It was Denise. "I asked my mom if you could come over tonight and she said you could."

"OK," I agreed, "but my aunt hasn't said anything about a meeting."

"Can she hear you?" Denise sounded worried.

"Nooo, I'm talking on my own phone."

"You lucky!"

I was laughing happily to myself when I returned to help Aunt Maggie. "Denise asked me to stay over at her house tonight," I told my aunt, making my face go straight. "Is that all right?"

She was concentrating on cutting the meat from a chicken leg. "It's fine. I'm going to have a private gathering at the river, and I was wondering what you would like to do." She emphasized the word "private."

Aha, she was having a witches' meeting in the full moon.

That evening in Denise's room, we had giggling fits making up stories for her mother so she'd let us go out in the woods. We decided on taping frog croaks for music class. Her mom bought it. Denise's dad raised his eyebrows, but he didn't say anything. When we left the house, Denise carried her tape recorder to make it look good.

Fortunately, the moonlight helped us find the path through the trees. As we grew close to the river, Denise and I moved more slowly, carefully avoiding crackling branches. When light glowed ahead of us, we crawled on our stomachs to the edge of the bank overlooking the clearing. What I saw below made my breath hiss through my teeth and into my chest.

Thirteen witches sat in a circle around a glowing pot. Each was bent over a cup she held in her hands. Candles flickered at the four corners behind their backs. Aunt Maggie stood at one side holding a large urn. Her voice was clear in the still night air. "As the shadows in our hearts drop into our cups, under the white moon, we are left cleansed and pure."

She lifted her cup toward the sky and called out, "As I will, so mote it be."

All the witches lifted their cups to the sky and repeated, "So mote it be."

Aunt Maggie went around the inside of the circle and

bent down so each witch could pour the contents of her cup into Aunt Maggie's urn. As the firelight shone on one witch's face, I thought she looked like Ms. Treble, and I nudged Denise.

After Aunt Maggie completed the circle, she took her full urn to the river and emptied it in the water. Another witch began beating on a single drumskin. The rest held hands and chanted words I couldn't understand.

"What are they saying?" I whispered to Denise.

"Who knows," Denise whispered back.

The chanting grew louder, and the drumbeats came faster. Just as my body was pulsing with the sounds, Aunt Maggie cried out, "Now!"

It felt like an explosion of energy flew into the air.

"Whoa!" I said.

"Too much," Denise said.

All the witches, except Aunt Maggie, bent forward, putting their hands flat on the ground. Aunt Maggie looked up at the bank.

Uh-oh. I wiggled backward. Denise wiggled with me. When we were about two yards from the edge of the bank, we got up and ran. Near the end of the woods, the strap on Denise's recorder caught on a branch and she fell down, with me tumbling after her. Denise yanked on the strap, and the branch broke and landed on top of us. We lay on the ground laughing until I took the branch and pointed it toward the sky. "I will go skating every Friday night. So mote it be!"

Denise grabbed the branch from me and pointed it

toward the moon. "I will get my own phone for my birthday. So mote it be!"

I snatched the branch back and started to say, "Aunt Dorothy will . . ." when I remembered that a curse returned three times stronger. "We better get going," I said instead.

As soon as we got in Denise's front door, her dad looked up from his book. "Well, let's hear the frog croaks."

Uh-oh. Denise closed the door slowly.

"The frog croaks?" Her dad repeated. Her mom was now looking at us, too. When Denise didn't say anything, her mother put down her crocheting.

"We were watching the witches," Denise said in a little voice.

"Denise!" her mother said in a big voice. "I told you those coven meetings were none of your business."

"What do you expect from twelve-year-olds?" Before her dad took up his book again, I thought I saw a smile flicker across his face.

Her mom wasn't smiling. "I don't want any trouble with our neighbors. And I don't want you snooping. And I hate lying."

Denise's head sunk into her shoulders. I didn't know if I should leave or not.

"Denise, do you understand that I want to be able to trust you?" Her mother was leaning forward in her chair.

The word "trust" circled around my head.

"Yes," Denise replied. "I'm sorry. We just wanted to see their ceremony. We didn't do any harm."

"You do me harm when you tell me stories."

"I'm really sorry, Mom."

I thought Denise was going to cry. I guess her mother thought she'd had enough scolding, too. "You girls go on to bed. It's past your bedtime, anyway."

I didn't sleep much. I kept thinking of trust and lies and knowing Aunt Maggie knew I was on the bank. Denise said no one could see who was there. But I said Aunt Maggie could.

In the morning, I felt miserable. I kept my head bent over my pancakes, except to ask Denise's dad to pass the syrup and to ask Denise's mom what "so mote it be" meant.

"It means," she said, " 'so it must be.' "

Right after breakfast, I hurried on down the road to Aunt Maggie's house. If she doesn't kick me out, I thought, from now on, I'll tell her the truth. I wondered where I'd go if I did get kicked out again. I couldn't depend on my mother. My feet dragged up the front steps of the house. I liked everyone here so much. Denise, Mrs. Thompson, Ms. Treble. And Aunt Maggie.

She was sitting on the davenport with her shoes off and her hands turned up in her lap—doing nothing. There was no expression on her face. I waited. She didn't move or say anything.

I let my tote bag drop to the floor. "Well, the Tarot cards were right, weren't they? You can't trust me."

130

She looked up at me then. "Did you remember that I said it was a private gathering?"

"Yes, and I didn't respect that."

"And you didn't respect me."

"I . . ." I did respect her, but I didn't have the words to explain it. In fact, I had thought she looked so queenlike in the moonlight. "I guess nobody can depend on me."

"You're not helpless, Copper," she said. "Anytime, you can decide how you want to be."

That's all she said. I didn't know what to do. I didn't know whether to go to my room or stay there with her. When I couldn't stand her calm silence any longer, I asked, "Are you going to dump me?"

"Why would I do that?"

I shrugged. "The Tarot cards said you couldn't trust me."

" 'For a little while.' You can change that whenever you want to."

I wanted to say I had been planning to change, but I didn't think that would help much. Instead, I picked up my bag and went to my room to do my homework. When Aunt Maggie called me for dinner, we ate together quietly, and afterward I did the dishes and made the kitchen shine.

Chapter
18

WHEN I CAME HOME FROM SCHOOL TUESDAY, THERE was a letter for me in the mailbox. I tore the envelope open as I went in the house. There was a check inside made out to Margo Jones for three hundred dollars. And a note to me.

Copper,
Your mother called and said you'd moved in with your father's sister. I'm enclosing a check to cover your room and board for the next three weeks.
Hang in there, babe.

Jeff

I gave the note and check to Aunt Maggie while we were eating dinner. "He doesn't say anything about Mom and me coming to Portland."

"No, he doesn't," Aunt Maggie said. "But maybe he'll help her get ready for a job."

I shook my head. "I don't know if she'd like that."

Aunt Maggie was flipping the check back and forth in her fingers. "I'm wondering what we should do with all the money. Probably the first thing you need is a warmer jacket."

"You're supposed to have all the money," I said.

She pointed the check at me. "To take care of you."

This was a new twist. I'm sure Aunt Dorothy never thought her check was to spend on me.

The phone rang then. It was my mom. She wanted to know if we'd heard from Jeff. I told her we had. She sounded kind of lonely, and before she hung up, she said, "I wish you were here, honey."

"Me, too," I said back, because I knew that was what she wanted me to say.

Before I went to sleep that night, I decided to try again to change my dreams. I said over and over to myself, "I will know I am dreaming when I dream. I will know I am dreaming when I dream."

I dreamed I was scrambling onto the back of a seaplane. The pilot started up the plane without waiting for me. While he taxied ahead in the water, I managed to climb aboard. The inside of the plane seemed more like a boat.

The pilot was in the front of a big room, behind him there were boxes and junk, and in the back there were a few chairs. There didn't seem to be enough chairs for the people. I stood for a while and then found a place on the floor. As we took off in the air, I felt twinges of fear and wished I had a book to read so I could ignore the flight.

We landed in Anchorage. I looked out the window (I was sitting in a chair now) and saw a forest landscape. I thought it was beautiful, but knew the sun wouldn't be shining often. When we took off again, I saw my mother on the plane. She was laughing with a strange man. Both the man and she were holding cocktail glasses. I went up to warn her against drinking. She put her arm around my shoulders and introduced me to the man. Then she seemed to forget me.

Next we landed in Petersburg. I wondered how many stops there'd be before we got to Sitka, our destination. It was cold in Petersburg, and snow was on the ground. I wished I had brought warmer clothes.

I found myself outside the plane, climbing up a hillside. I was quite a distance away from where the plane had docked. It occurred to me that I might miss the plane's takeoff. I hurried down the hill to the buildings on the dock. When I looked through the window of one of the buildings, I saw the plane slipping slowly away in the water. Frantically, I banged a door open and shut, trying to get the pilot's attention.

I wondered how I was ever going to catch up to the plane. I worried about being stranded. I watched the plane go out farther in the water, moving away from the buildings.

Suddenly I realized I was on the plane and no longer stranded. This is a dream, I thought, and I don't have to be stranded. I can be on the plane.

The plane was larger now, and there were many more

people on it. I had to go to the bathroom and looked all over for a lavatory door, but couldn't find one.

That was when I woke up. I had to go to the bathroom, all right. While I was sitting on the toilet, I thought, wow, I did it! I knew I was dreaming in a dream.

When I told Aunt Maggie my dream at the breakfast table, she was proud of me. Her eyes got all shiny. She told me it was a wonderful dream.

"Well, I only knew I was dreaming in part of it," I said.

"But you made a change."

I nodded. Then I came out with something that had been worrying and worrying me. "Do you think my mom will really stop drinking this time?"

"I don't know. Only your mother can decide what she's going to do."

I stirred my spoon around in my oatmeal, not really feeling very hungry.

"Copper." Aunt Maggie looked right in my eyes to get my attention. "Do you like living here?"

"Sure I do." What did she think?

"Would you like to stay with me until your mother gets settled and have this place as your home whenever you wanted it?"

"Really?" I stared back at her in amazement. "After I spied on you?"

"I don't think that was the biggest sin in the world. And I enjoy you. You're a resourceful, self-reliant girl. Intelligent, curious about life, and not the least bit lazy."

"And I lie and I manipulate people."

"You changed your dream. You can change yourself any way you want." She got up from the table. "And we'd better get moving or we're both going to be late."

I stood up, too. "Do witches give hugs?"

"Witches love hugs." She reached out her round arms and squashed my skinny self against her soft body. When she let me go, I was blinking fast to keep from crying. She ruffled my hair. "You're all right, Copper," she said.

I hopped down the road to meet Denise, my school books flopping at my side. I was thinking about changes and who I'd like to be like. Would I like to be like Mrs. Thompson, who everybody loved? And go to a white church with a belfry and spire?

Or would I like to be a witch with little powers? But, I thought, what if I'm walking along the road to a coven meeting and I bump into Ricky Layton?

"Hey, there, Copper," he'd say.

"Hi," I'd say.

"What's with that black kettle you're carrying?" he'd say.

Then what would I say?